Robbie rubbed at the side of her nose, leaving a chocolate smear. Joel could resist chocolate smears on her nose. Just…

She gave the wooden spatula another couple of turns in the bowl and then pushed a stray curl out of her eyes. That was plain irresistible.

"You've got chocolate in your hair. No…don't touch, let me…" Robbie had just managed to add another smear to her forehead. Joel strode toward her, grinning.

He managed to wipe most of the gooey mixture from her hair, but he couldn't stop himself from wiping her forehead with his fingers and taking a taste.

"The frosting's good."

Then he was lost in her gaze, pale sapphire tonight under the bright kitchen lights. Robbie's mouth curled into a mischievous grin.

"That's not enough to tell, is it?" She dipped her finger in the bowl, holding her hand up toward him.

A rich, chocolaty taste on his tongue and the feel of her body against his as she stepped closer. Then Joel did what he'd been aching to do since the first moment he'd seen Robbie, and kissed her.

Dear Reader,

One of the nice things about living anywhere for any length of time is finding its hidden gems. I've lived in London for many years, and stumbled across quite a few examples of "Secret London"—places that tourists never get to see but which are appreciated and enjoyed by local people.

So in writing a book about secrets, where better to set it than in Secret London? I'd walked past more than one Tin Tabernacle without really noticing these strange and interesting buildings, but when I did find out a little more about them their history fascinated me. A renovated Tin Tabernacle seemed a perfect base for Dr. Robbie Hall's charity Nightshifters, and the building also serves as a center for the riverside community that surrounds it.

When Dr. Joel Mason volunteers to work with Nightshifters he becomes part of the Tin Tabernacle's close-knit community. But as Joel and Robbie find themselves falling for each other, can they move past the personal secrets that have shaped both of their lives that threaten to keep them apart?

Thank you for reading Robbie and Joel's story!

Annie x

FROM THE NIGHT SHIFT TO FOREVER

———

ANNIE CLAYDON

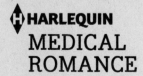

HARLEQUIN

MEDICAL
ROMANCE

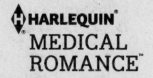

MEDICAL ROMANCE™

Recycling programs
for this product may
not exist in your area.

ISBN-13: 978-1-335-40914-0

From the Night Shift to Forever

Copyright © 2022 by Annie Claydon

This edition published by arrangement with Harlequin Books S.A.

For questions and comments about the quality of this book,
please contact us at CustomerService@Harlequin.com.

Harlequin Enterprises ULC
22 Adelaide St. West, 41st Floor
Toronto, Ontario M5H 4E3, Canada
www.Harlequin.com

Printed in U.S.A.

Cursed with a poor sense of direction and a propensity to read, **Annie Claydon** spent much of her childhood lost in books. A degree in English literature followed by a career in computing didn't lead directly to her perfect job—writing romance for Harlequin—but she has no regrets in taking the scenic route. She lives in London: a city where getting lost can be a joy.

Books by Annie Claydon

Harlequin Medical Romance

Dolphin Cove Vets
Healing the Vet's Heart

London Heroes
Falling for Her Italian Billionaire
Second Chance with the Single Mom

Winning the Surgeon's Heart
A Rival to Steal Her Heart
The Best Man and the Bridesmaid
Greek Island Fling to Forever
Falling for the Brooding Doc
The Doctor's Reunion to Remember
Risking It All for a Second Chance

Visit the Author Profile page
at Harlequin.com for more titles.

To Maggie, with thanks for tea and inspiration!

**Praise for
Annie Claydon**

"A spellbinding contemporary medical romance that will keep readers riveted to the page, *Festive Fling with Single Dad* is a highly enjoyable treat from Annie Claydon's immensely talented pen."

—*Goodreads*

CHAPTER ONE

IT WAS JUST another Friday night in A & E. Busy, sometimes frustrating, sometimes heart-rending. Tears, drunkenness and pain. But Dr Joel Mason wasn't in any doubt that this was exactly where he wanted to be. He was hoping an angel might arrive at any moment.

North London Nightshifters was a local charity and one of the first things he'd been told about when he started work here, six weeks ago. If you were running low on something, they'd find it for you and deliver it. They worked at nights when the usual supply chains weren't operating, and an emergency case might otherwise mean a set of frantic phone calls, trying to locate what you needed and get it sent over via a taxi service. Many of their couriers were medical professionals, and so they were able to check their cargo and get it to the right place with the minimum of fuss and the maximum of care.

He'd seen the couriers a few times already, coming in and out of the hospital. Two of them had been noticeable only for the Nightshifters logo on their courier bags, but the third had made him turn and look. A woman in motorcycle leathers, with blonde curls and pale skin, ethereal and glowing. Her smile was almost formidably bright, like a warrior angel's...

His phone buzzed in his pocket. It really didn't much matter which courier was coming, just as long as they were here. Nightshifters had located the blood he needed, which in itself was nothing short of a miracle since his current patient had such a rare blood group that most hospitals didn't carry stocks of it.

'It's here.' He turned to the nurse who had been monitoring the young woman he was treating. 'I'll go and collect it.'

He opened the door of the cubicle, just in time to see her. His thanks dried in his throat as the box was shoved into his hands, and the courier took off her motorcycle helmet, her blonde curls falling around her face. He could see now that she had sapphire-blue eyes.

'Don't just stand there.' Her voice had a melodic quality about it and betrayed more than a trace of humour. 'Check and sign.' She unzipped her jacket, producing a docket.

Joel opened the box, looking inside, checking that the quantity and blood type were correct. Then he took the paperwork, scanning it and scribbling his name at the bottom.

'Thanks. You're a lifesaver.'

'That's the general plan.' She gave him the merest hint of a smile and then turned her back on him and walked away.

Joel hesitated for one moment, resisting the urge to run after her and ask her name. Then he too turned, taking the lifesaving cargo back with him into the cubicle.

Robbie Hall walked back out of the A & E department, signalling a goodbye to the receptionist. Then she unzipped one of the pockets of her leather jacket, taking out her phone.

'Hello, Nightshifters, how can we help?'

'You can tell me I don't have any more calls for tonight, Glen.'

Glen's low chuckle sounded in her ear. 'Nah, we're done. Haven't you seen the time?'

The traffic on the roads had gone from non-existent to light as she'd made her way here, and the sun had been up for a while. Robbie took a guess.

'About seven o'clock?'

'Nearer eight. And you've finished for the night. We've no more calls.'

'Great, thanks. I'm going to the cafeteria to get some breakfast.'

'You caught up with the new doctor?'

There wasn't any particular doubt about where Glen was going with the question. In addition to daylighting as a paediatric physiotherapist and moonlighting at Nightshifters, Glen was a confirmed matchmaker. Lately he seemed to be viewing Robbie as his most troublesome challenge.

'Two heads. Breath that would make a dragon faint, and I thought I spotted a tail under his white coat…' Robbie sent up a silent apology for the undeserved injury to Dr Mason's reputation.

'You're far too picky, Rob. Breakfast for two makes you see someone in a completely different light…'

Breakfast for two wasn't on Robbie's agenda. Not this morning or any morning. She'd seen Dr Joel Mason from afar, when he'd been given a whistle-stop tour of the paediatric A & E unit. A couple of the nurses who'd had the benefit of an introduction had told her his name and that he was the new doctor for general A & E, confirming at some length that he looked just as good close up as he did at a distance. Robbie could now privately confirm their assessment, but that was as far as it went.

'I'm not thinking about getting lucky at this moment. I'm too hungry. Want me to bring you an egg-and-bacon sandwich?'

'He'd be the one getting lucky, Rob. And no thanks to the sandwich, Carla's packed me soup and pasties.'

'Stop. Right now…' Glen's wife was a great cook and Robbie's stomach began to growl with envy.

'They smell pretty good. Even better when I warm them up in the microwave…'

'I'm hanging up, Glen. Actually, I'm never speaking to you again, so have a nice life…' Robbie heard Glen's laughter as she ended the call.

The staff in the cafeteria were getting ready for the morning onslaught as the night shift came off duty. The toast was freshly made and when Pete saw the motorcycle helmet and leathers, he gave her extra bacon and eggs done the way she liked them.

'Had a good night, Dr Hall?'

'You've just made it a great night, thanks, Pete. A large coffee would round it off perfectly.'

Pete had the coffee ready and put it onto her tray, waving her away from the cash register. 'It turns out that one of your visits last week was for the daughter of a posh bloke. He got in touch with the chairman of the hospital board and he's set up a tab for the Nightshifters.'

Robbie nodded. The posh bloke was an MP and his daughter had needed a ventilator. 'Use the tab for the others—I'll pay.'

Pete looked affronted. 'I've worked out a rota and everyone gets three free breakfasts. Don't mess with my system.'

Upsetting Pete's system was more important than Robbie's embarrassment at being well able to afford to pay. She grinned, picking up her tray. 'Okay, thanks, then. I'll enjoy this even more.'

A table in one corner was free and she sat down, peeling off the thin protective gloves she wore underneath her motor cycle gloves. The small patch of eczema on the back of her hand was fading fast and didn't itch at all now. And an egg-and-bacon sandwich was like a taste of heaven at the moment.

By the time she got to coffee, Robbie was beginning to relax. She'd go home and sleep, then let the rest of her Saturday take its course. Maybe spend a bit of time cooking, instead of just pulling something out of the freezer. She'd taken up cooking as her new and relaxing hobby, and if the results weren't always great the making of mess and then cleaning it up again did the trick for the relaxing part. It was all sounding pretty perfect when a shadow blocked the light from the window and made her look up.

He really *was* handsome. Or, on closer inspection, not quite perfectly handsome, because then he would have had a symmetrical smile. The crooked grin that Joel Mason was giving her now was far, far more attractive than perfect features could ever be.

'Hi. May I join you?'

She'd almost finished her breakfast so it would only be for a few minutes. Robbie leaned forward, catching her motorcycle helmet up from the seat opposite and tucking it next to her on the bench.

'Sure. How's your patient?'

'Looking a lot better now. She'd lost a lot of blood and we were keeping her stable with fluids. Now we can risk sending her down for surgery to set her broken leg.'

His dark-eyed gaze seemed to be pulling her in, to a place of warmth. Robbie struggled to escape it and didn't quite succeed. The mental effort was unsettling, because it made her want to jump to her feet and move, rather than just watch as he sat down and unloaded his tray onto the table.

'Great. We're here to help.' Robbie toyed

with the last crust of her sandwich, trying to use it to divert her attention.

'I'm new here. Joel Mason.' He reached across the table and Robbie picked up her coffee, nodding a *hello* instead of shaking his outstretched hand. Don't touch what you can't have…

'I know. Robbie Hall. I work in the paediatric A & E department.'

'Here? I'm sorry, you must be one of the million people I was introduced to.' He shook his head slightly, as if wondering how he could have forgotten.

'We weren't introduced. I saw you from the other side of the room.'

That sounded as if she'd been staring at him across rooms. The slight quirk of Joel's lips didn't help Robbie's discomfiture. 'I was dealing with a four-year-old boy who'd swallowed a twenty-pence piece.'

'Was he okay?' The medical detail was enough to divert his attention.

'Yes, we X-rayed him and it was in his stomach. When he came back a few days later for another X-ray it was gone.' Robbie took a sip of her coffee and Joel grinned suddenly.

'I imagine you see that kind of thing more often in Paediatrics than we do in general A & E.' He picked up his knife and fork and started to tuck into the full English breakfast in front of him. 'I'm interested in Nightshifters…'

That was good to hear. It took her mind off Joel's square jaw and broad shoulders. His thick dark hair, cut short, which lent a touch of the unyielding to his soft, mesmerising eyes. And it was always nice when someone expressed an interest in Nightshifters because Robbie had put a lot of work into setting it up, and she financed most of its costs from her trust fund. It was her creation, although she didn't want any credit for that, preferring to stay in the background and get on with the things she really wanted to do. Apart from Glen, even the volunteers didn't know that Robbie provided most of the funding.

'You're thinking of helping us out?' She might as well throw a challenge his way.

Joel's fork paused in mid-air, halfway towards his mouth. 'Maybe. What do you need?'

Good question. It was the one that the Nightshifters always asked. 'Lots of things. People with some medical knowledge, who can find their way around the system and track down whatever's needed. Drivers, who can check the consignment they're carrying and make sure it's right. It helps if you know London as well—we don't usually have the time for getting lost.'

'And that's what you do? Someone like me calls you and asks for something, and you track it down and deliver it.'

'It's slightly different with blood—there are established channels that we use. At night we can often transport what's needed quicker and more reliably, so that an urgent request like yours doesn't have to rely on a regular taxi service. We're not the only charity doing work of this kind, there are different groups all around the country. We're locally based and serve the hospitals in this area.'

'What hours do you work?'

'We're open from eight at night until eight in the morning, but everyone gives what time they can. I usually do either a whole night, or midnight until eight in the morning, because I work nights at the hospital. People who work days tend to prefer eight in the evening until midnight.'

'How many nights a week?'

'I work one, sometimes two. But Glen, our coordinator, makes sure that no one takes on more than they can comfortably sustain. Everyone has commitments and a lot of people do just one night every two weeks or a month.' When she said it like that, it sounded as if she didn't have a life outside the hospital during the week and Nightshifters at the weekends. That was largely true.

If that had occurred to Joel, then he wasn't saying. If he was *really* interested in helping out, then they could always do with more volunteers. Robbie would just have to forgive him the good looks and the stomach-stirring sensuality.

'And…you use motorbikes?'

'That's just me, actually. The charity owns a couple of cars for deliveries, but a lot of people prefer to use their own and claim a mileage allowance. A lot of our delivery teams work in pairs.'

He grinned suddenly. 'But not you.'

'I prefer to work alone.' And the bike was a pretty good excuse for Robbie to do so.

He nodded, slicing into the toast on the side of his plate, and dipping a piece of it into the runny yolk of the eggs. Robbie waited as he chewed thoughtfully, and then gave in to her own impatience and asked the question that meant rather more to her than it should.

'So, are you interested?'

'I'd definitely like to know more.'

Good answer. In Robbie's experience it was the people who wanted to know more before committing themselves who were really interested in helping. Plenty of people promised a lot, on the basis of a five-minute conversation, and then you never saw them again.

'Then you should speak to Glen. He's the boss.' That was true, in terms of the day-to-day running of the operation. Glen had known Robbie's father for years, working with him on a number of charitable projects, and he knew how wealthy Robbie's family was. When Robbie had first started to develop her idea for Nightshifters, Dad had introduced her to Glen and they made a great team. He'd accepted Robbie's offer to run North London Nightshifters, and allowed her to make her own safe place there, where she was valued for what she could contribute on a practical basis, rather than how much money she could spend.

'And how do I get in contact with him?'

'I can get him to call you. Or you're welcome to pop into the office and see for yourself what we do.'

'I'm free this evening. Any time after eight.'

Joel didn't waste any time in putting his decisions into action. But Saturday night was a good time to come because Nightshifters was always busy and he'd see some of the challenges of what they did. And Robbie was planning to be in the office, as well.

'This evening's fine. Glen's expected at nine,

so that's the best time to come. I'll be there too, so I can show you around.' She reached into her jacket for her notepad, writing down the instructions to get to the office. That was generally the second stumbling block. If Joel could find his way to the office, then he was serious.

'Great, thanks. I'll see you later on this evening.' He folded the paper without looking at it and put it into his pocket.

Robbie emptied her coffee cup, gathering up her jacket and helmet, ready to go. 'Yeah. See you later.'

It was the strangest address that Joel had ever seen. He'd gone home and slept for eight hours, then found the piece of paper that Robbie had given him. Then he'd puzzled over it for a while, and decided that the only way he was going to arrive was by starting out.

Orton Road was easy, ten minutes' walk from the Underground stop before the one for the hospital. Joel walked to the end of the road as instructed, and then turned left onto a footpath that led between a high wall and the side of the last house in the street. Then right onto a footbridge that spanned a small waterway, one of the tributaries of the Thames.

The steps at the other side of the bridge led

down onto a wide riverside path, well lit and still busy, with a row of narrowboats moored on one side. Joel consulted the instructions again.

Walk down until you get to a corrugated iron building, painted turquoise.

Now that he was actually here, a corrugated iron building painted turquoise didn't sound quite so impossible. He'd driven across the road bridge a little further down many times, and was vaguely aware of the fact that there were boats here. But this looked like a whole community, living in the heart of London and yet to all intents and purposes hidden. Joel kept walking and caught sight of a flash of colour up ahead, set back from the river path.

The one-storey building, with a pitched roof and a small porch over the door at the front, was painted a particularly bright shade of turquoise. As he got closer, it also looked as if it were made entirely of corrugated iron, but there was an arched wooden door, and the windows that stretched along the side had wooden frames and shutters. Joel had never seen anything quite like it, and the overall effect was both odd and enchanting.

There was a sign beside the door bearing

the charity's name, and, reassured that he was in the right place, he reached forward and knocked on the front door. He could hear the sounds of activity inside, and was just wondering whether he should wait or go inside when the door was flung open suddenly. Robbie was wearing a pair of jeans and a chunky knitted red sweater, which swamped her slim frame. Her hair curled around the side of her face, and she had a pencil propped behind her ear. The effect was enchanting and not even slightly odd.

'Hi. Don't bother about knocking, no one ever does. You made it, then?' She stood back from the doorway, and let him into a large, open-plan space. Lights hung from wooden beams that supported the V-shape of the roof, and the walls were clad in white painted timber panels. She was quite alone, but the comfortable seating and the two L-shaped desks at the far end of the space indicated that the office was designed to hold more than just one person.

'I said I would. What *is* this place?'

Robbie grinned, shutting the door behind him. 'It's a Tin Tabernacle. Haven't you seen one before?'

'No. You mean there's more than one of these?'

She laughed suddenly. Joel wanted more of that. Her laughter seemed to brighten the well-lit space around her.

'They were built in the mid- to late-eighteen hundreds and designed to provide low-cost churches and community halls, which could be taken down and put back up again to follow moving communities, such as construction workers on the rail and canal networks.'

'Hence the wooden doors and windows.' Joel turned to inspect the door. It was solid oak, and the dents and scratches were obviously touches of character that had been developed over many years.

'Yes, they all have these really good quality doors. If they're well maintained they'll last for ever. This one was used as a community hall and it's on brick footings so it's survived pretty well. We were lucky to get it. They're in quite a bit of demand as architectural curiosities, but the owners put a condition on the sale that said it had to be used for community purposes.'

'And they let you paint it turquoise?' It was a great colour, fitting in with the characterful nature of the building, but Joel wondered what the historians might think of that.

'They're all painted in these bright colours. Yellow, sky blue…a lot of them are various shades of turquoise—it's all part of their charm…' The phone rang and Robbie's head spun around. 'Uh, hang on a minute. Make yourself comfortable.'

She shot over to one of the desks, answering the phone. Joel sat down on one of the comfortable sofas, looking up as two men entered.

'Hi. You're Robbie's doctor?' One of them came forward, holding out his hand, and Joel got to his feet to shake it.

It would be nice to be Robbie's anything and doctor would do for starters. Joel dismissed the thought, because belonging with someone had never been one of his goals. A wide and varied group of friends, colleagues and acquaintances was a good thing. Friends with benefits was an occasional option, but anything approaching a real relationship took a great deal more trust than he was comfortable with.

'I'm Joel Mason. I work in A & E at the London Fitzrovia hospital and I met Robbie briefly this morning, when she brought some blood supplies we needed.'

'Glen Taverner, I'm a paediatric physiotherapist over at St Stephen's Hospital. And that's Dan Wright, he works at St Stephen's too.' Glen jerked his thumb towards the other man, who signalled a hello.

Glen was tall and bulky, the kind of guy that

looked as if he could dead-lift the average person. But he had the gentle air and ready smile that most kids responded to.

'You have a great set-up here. And you came to my rescue this morning.'

Glen chuckled. 'That's the general plan. You're thinking of joining us?'

Joel didn't get a chance to answer. Robbie put the phone down, calling over to them.

'Guys, sorry… I know you've only just got here but I've got someone from St Stephen's who needs some milk for a preemie baby.'

'I'll go.' Glen responded to Robbie and then turned to Joel. 'Sorry about this, but Dan's just done three deliveries without a break, so I should do this one. If you'd like to leave your contact details, I can get in touch with you during the week.'

'We can talk later, maybe. I was hoping to be able to see a bit of what goes on here, if that's okay?' Joel replied.

'You're welcome to stay as long as you like.' Glen turned towards Robbie, grinning at her. 'Robbie can tell you all you need to know.'

Glen walked over to the desk, putting down the large plastic food box he was carrying, and taking the docket that Robbie had just filled out from her hand.

'Thanks, Glen.' Robbie tapped the box with

her finger. 'Carla hasn't sent coffee and wal-nut cake, has she?'

'Yep. And if it's all gone by the time I get back, I'll know who to blame.'

'You'd better hurry up, then.' Robbie chuck-led, turning to Joel. 'Glen's wife, Carla, is *the* most amazing cook. I love her coffee and wal-nut cake.'

'There's banana bread in there too...' Glen was halfway to the door, waving over his shoulder. 'Never say that I don't do anything for you.'

'Tell Carla that if she ever gets tired of you, I'll marry her,' Dan called after him, and Glen's easy laugh sounded as he closed the door behind him.

'Right, then.' Robbie turned to Joel. 'Coffee and walnut cake or banana bread?'

'Banana bread.' He felt in his pocket. 'Is there a kitty for cakes?'

'No, that's okay, you can put your money away until January. We have a whip-round for Carla's birthday and I only take notes.' She grinned. 'The board makes sure that Glen and Carla aren't out of pocket for all the baking she does for us.'

'Okay, thanks. There's a board in charge of all of this?'

'Every charity has to have a board of trustees. But Glen's the one who's actually in charge here—whatever he says, goes. While we're waiting for him to get back, I'll show you the ropes and then you can talk to him about whether you want to join us or not.'

There wasn't really any question about that. Joel had already seen the difference that the Nightshifters were making, and the easy camaraderie here made him feel instantly at home. And then there was the added bonus of Robbie's smile.

He was already sold. He wanted to be a part of this.

It was turning into a busy night. The three women and five men who were on courier duty tonight barely had time to introduce themselves to Joel and grab a coffee before they were sent back out again. Robbie was expecting him to just watch, and wait until Glen returned, but instead he came to sit at the desk next to hers and offered to take over the phones while she located some equipment that was needed by one of the hospitals in the area.

He was still there at midnight, when the pressure suddenly lifted and there was a lull in the calls. Joel stood up, stretching his shoulders, and Robbie tried not to look at him. She reckoned she'd done a fine job of pretending not to notice when his fingers brushed hers as he passed the call information across to her to distribute amongst the drivers. But the way he'd snatched his hand back made it very clear that he'd noticed, and that he knew all about keeping his distance.

Everyone had their own reason for working nights, but maybe Joel's were the same as hers. There wasn't too much time for meeting people and if you did then the unsocial hours were enough to keep things uncomplicated. It seemed that Joel shared her reservations about acknowledging the moments when two desks hadn't been a significant enough barrier to prevent Robbie from feeling that she was falling into the warmth of his gaze.

'Shall I make coffee?' He grinned at her.

'You're a…' Sweetheart? Tower of strength? The available evidence was indicating that he was both, and that he could probably be a great lover as well. 'Good timing. I could murder a coffee right now.'

Joel glanced around, including the four drivers who were sitting in the easy chairs in his offer, and took their orders. Glen ambled over towards her, sitting down on the other side of the desk and planting his elbows on it.

'Is this a volunteer opportunity? Or a date?' He murmured the words so quietly that even

Robbie could hardly hear him. Joel was at the far end of the office, chatting amiably with Rosie as she showed him how to operate the cappuccino machine, so there was no chance that he could be privy to the conversation.

'I've known him ten minutes. It's a volunteer opportunity.'

Glen grinned. 'When I met Carla it took me about ninety seconds to know.'

'That's you and Carla, you were made for each other. If I ever had a Prince Charming, I think he must have left my glass slipper on the train on his way home.'

'Lost Property's always an option.' Robbie waved Glen's suggestion away, and he abandoned it. 'Whatever. So you'll ask Joel if he can join us?'

'That's up to you. You're the North London coordinator.' Robbie pressed her lips together. She didn't want to have anything to do with asking Joel to stay, because she wanted him to so much.

'You're the founder, Rob. And our largest source of funding…' Glen practically mouthed the words at her, careful that none of the other volunteers should hear.

'And you're in charge, Glen.'

Robbie had said it enough times, but Glen was never slow in voicing the opinion that she should at least take some credit for her involvement. But he knew that Robbie was more comfortable with the way things were, and he went along with it.

'If you're so intent on me being the boss, then I should remind you that I'm allowed to delegate, Rob.'

Robbie shot him a smile. 'But you're so much better at it than I am, Glen.'

Glen clearly wasn't convinced. He flapped his hand dismissively, muttering something about excuses as he got to his feet. Walking over to Joel, he started to chat to him, and, while Rosie took the coffees back to the group in the seating area, the two men seemed deep in conversation. Finally they shook hands, and Joel walked back to the desk next to Robbie's.

'Looks as if I'm on the team.' His grin told Robbie that he was pleased about that, and she felt a shiver run down her spine.

'That's great.' She smiled across at Glen, who had taken a moment to speak to one of the other drivers and was now heading back towards them. 'When are you starting?'

'I've got to get a copy of my driving licence and various other documents to Glen first, so he can do the paperwork, but he says next weekend would be fine.'

Glen joined them. 'I'd like you to take Joel

in hand and show him how everything works, if you would, Robbie. Since you'll be here next weekend.'

Glen didn't give up on an idea... But Robbie had told him that he was the boss, and she could hardly veto any of his decisions now. And something about the melting look in Joel's eyes made her feel that she wouldn't mind taking him in hand one bit.

'Next Saturday, then...?'

Both Joel and Glen nodded, and suddenly the gap between now and next Saturday opened up into a wide chasm. Robbie reminded herself that counting days before she saw Joel again wasn't on her agenda.

The phone rang and she reached for it. But Joel was quicker, grabbing it and giving her a delicious smile as he answered. 'Hello, Night-shifters. How can we help?'

CHAPTER TWO

RESISTING THE TEMPTATION to walk over to the Paediatric A & E department to find Robbie, was made a great deal easier by knowing that he'd be spending the night with her next Saturday.

Spending the night… He shouldn't really think of it as that; maybe working a shift was a better way of looking at it. Learning something from her. Even the word *learning* was problematic, because, despite Robbie's very obvious attitude that she was interested in him only as a fellow volunteer, he reckoned that she could teach him a few things about softness. About the yielding nature of a kiss…

But Joel wasn't up for yielding to that kind of thing, he never had been. He'd learned that particular lesson young, finding out that his father was unfaithful when he was only seven years old. He'd been sworn to silence, and told that if he didn't keep the secret from his mother, his family would break in two and it would all be *his* fault.

So he'd stayed silent. By the time he'd been able to apply an adult mind to the matter, it was a completely different decision. What was the point of hurting his mother with the revelation that his father had been unfaithful more than ten years ago?

But the torment hadn't ended. There had been times when he hadn't gone home because he couldn't face his mother and brother, and didn't want to face his father. When his mother had died suddenly, during his second year at medical school, guilt had made grief so much harder to bear. He'd lost precious time with his mother, and he'd lost the chance to make things right now.

The practice of medicine had filled the void in his heart. The secret that he kept meant that he hardly saw his own family, and he didn't feel qualified to make a new one for himself. Working at night was an easy way to keep his relationships uncomplicated and he'd taken the new job at the London Fitzrovia hospital on the understanding that the night shift was where he was most needed.

But when he'd seen Robbie he'd known that a short-lived affair with no strings attached wasn't going to work as a modus operandi this time. And that was going to be a problem.

He could convince himself that he'd volunteered because he wanted to be involved with the good work that Nightshifters were doing, and he had some time to spare. But as he came off shift on Friday morning, he couldn't truthfully tell himself that the excitement in the pit of his stomach wasn't something to do with seeing Robbie again.

As he wearily walked to his locker, his phone rang. Joel glanced at the screen and answered, expecting that Glen had thought of yet another piece of paper he needed to bring with him this evening, to keep the records straight.

'Hi, Joel. Are you still at work?' Glen sounded unusually terse.

'Yes, just finishing. What can I do for you?'

'I need a favour. Robbie's come off her bike at the side entrance to the hospital. She called saying she was all right and she's making her way there on foot with a delivery but she didn't sound all right to me. I don't suppose—'

'I'll find her and call you back.' Joel ended the call, hurrying out of the staff exit and scanning the curved slip road that led from the side entrance of the hospital to A & E.

He saw her almost immediately, just yards away from the main entrance, walking slowly past one of the ambulances that was parked up outside. A courier bag was looped across one shoulder and her crash helmet was nowhere to be seen. Her other arm was hanging limp against her body.

Joel reached her at a run, and she looked up at him as if she'd been caught doing something she shouldn't.

'Hey. Glen said you came off your bike. Where's your crash helmet?' If she'd lost it or it had been damaged, she needed to stop moving around, right now.

'I took it off. No head injuries.'

That was no substitute for a proper examination, but it put his mind at rest a little. The next, most obvious area of concern was her shoulder, and he gently took the courier bag from her other shoulder. That seemed to afford her some relief and she straightened a little.

'Take it inside…' She still seemed to be struggling to stay on her feet.

The delivery was of secondary importance right now. But when he quickly looped the bag across his chest and held out his arm to support her she drew back, wincing as she did so, her hand flying protectively to her shoulder.

'Take the bag, Joel. I'll follow you in.'

She was obviously hurt and very probably

in shock. Sometimes the direct approach was the best one.

'Do I need to remind you who's in charge here? Take my arm, it's just a couple of steps. Can you manage that?' He spoke as kindly as he could, but he wasn't going to allow any arguments.

'Yes.' She was surveying the short distance from here to the main doors as if every inch was going to be a challenge and she took his arm, gripping it tightly. That more than anything convinced Joel that she really wasn't okay. He walked her slowly through the automatic doors, and carefully sat her down in the first available chair.

'Give them the bag, Joel.'

It was obvious that the sooner he made the delivery, the sooner Robbie would allow him to tend to her. He consulted the label attached to the parcel she'd brought, finding that it was milk for a premature baby, and hurried over to the reception desk. The receptionist asked him to wait, and Joel rapped out a brisk instruction for the woman to take charge of the delivery herself, and make sure that it got to the right place. Then he turned back to Robbie.

'My bike...'

She was blinking away tears, and cradling her arm against her body. Apparently this was the next thing on her list of concerns before he would be allowed to examine her.

'Stay there.' Joel hurried to fetch a wheel-chair, and when he returned Robbie's eyebrows shot up as if this were the first time in her life she'd ever seen such a thing.

'I can walk.'

'Hospital regulations.' Joel had no idea what the hospital regulations said about recalcitrant doctors on their way into A & E, but perhaps his no-nonsense tone did the trick. Robbie took his arm and stood, then sank into the wheel-chair and allowed him to wheel her through to a spare cubicle in the treatment area.

'Should we be going straight in?' Robbie was still in distress, but couldn't conceal her relief at being in a safe place now.

'My medical opinion is that you need to be seen straight away. There's nothing more urgent on the board, and I'm not on duty any more. Wait one minute while I call Glen and then we can forget all about everything apart from your arm.'

He pulled out his phone, and dialled Glen's mobile number. He answered on the first ring.

'Yep?'

'I've got Robbie here in A & E, she's taken a tumble and I'm going to examine her now.

The delivery's at Reception and Robbie's worried about her bike...'

'Okay, I'll call the special care baby unit, and make sure they know the delivery's there. Tell Rob not to worry about the bike, I've already got someone on the way and we'll deal with it.'

'Great. Thanks.'

'And don't take any nonsense from her, Joel. She's to shut up and follow doctor's orders...'

'Sure thing.' Joel ignored Robbie's outstretched hand, her fingers signalling that she wanted to talk to Glen, and ended the call.

'What did he say?' Robbie looked a little annoyed with him.

'Someone's already on their way to see to your bike and he's calling the recipient of the package to let them know it's here.'

She let out a shaky sigh, and allowed him to check her pulse. 'And the last part?'

'He...hopes you're okay.'

Robbie smirked suddenly. 'He definitely didn't say that.'

'No, actually. He said I should tell you to shut up and follow doctor's orders. Stop fighting me, Robbie.'

Tears welled in her eyes. She was beginning to let go, and she was obviously hurting badly. Before he turned his attention to her shoulder,

Joel performed a few quick checks to make sure there wasn't anything more serious going on here, trying to ignore the fact that she was weeping silently.

But it tore at his heart. He'd just let her in to the place he reserved for the hurt and the helpless, and there was no denying that Robbie could cause havoc there. But it was too late to go back now and she needed him.

'Am I going to ask, or will you just give me the answers?' He murmured the question, trying to regain some distance. Robbie knew what he needed to know, and having her just tell him was a way of checking how alert she was, as well.

'Someone hit me from behind and I went over the handlebars. I didn't hit my head and my leathers saved me from scrapes but I landed on my right shoulder...' She tailed off, vulnerability sounding in her voice.

Joel nodded. 'Anything else?'

Her eyes were focussed on his raised finger, following its movements. 'That's all, Joel. I *said* I hadn't hit my head.'

'Who's in charge here?'

She glared at him. 'I'll allow you to think that you are.'

'That's good, thanks. Let's see if I can get your jacket off without hurting you too much.'

He would have preferred another smart answer but Robbie nodded quietly. The fact that she had no more fight left in her was the symptom that concerned him the most, and he carefully unzipped her heavy jacket.

If this was what he thought it was, then pain was the most obvious symptom. She was wearing a loose-fitting hoodie underneath, and Joel unzipped that too, thanking his lucky stars that Robbie hadn't chosen to wear anything that he'd have to pull over her head. She knew what he had to do and he saw her press her lips together.

'We'll take it slow and steady. Uninjured arm first.' He helped her slip her left arm out of the jacket and hoodie together, revealing a white fitted T-shirt with long sleeves underneath.

'Well done. Now hold onto me to steady yourself if you need to...'

This was the part that would hurt the most, and he caught her left hand, resting it on his shoulder. Joel gritted his teeth, trying to insulate himself from the whimpers of pain that escaped her lips as he carefully loosened her jacket and hoodie from her right shoulder and threaded the sleeves down her arm.

The heavy jacket crumpled onto the floor and she was still holding onto him, her fingers bunching the material of his scrubs. She let go suddenly, turning her head away from him as if she was trying to conceal her tears. Joel resisted the temptation to comfort her, knowing that making this as quick and efficient as he could was the best way of ending it. He gently probed her shoulder with his fingers, and found what the slight droop of her shoulder had already indicated to him.

'I think your shoulder is partially dislocated and I'll order an X-ray to confirm. But I'm going to need to take a look at it. How fond of that T-shirt are you?'

Robbie nodded, as if that was what she'd expected to hear. 'Will you cut it, please?'

Joel nodded, smiling. 'Yeah, I think that's best.'

He'd been unable to stop thinking about Robbie in the last week, and he wouldn't have been surprised to find that he felt some trickle of the desire that had been threatening to wrap its web around him. Maybe it was their surroundings, but it was also her vulnerability and her tears that left him with nothing but the urgent need to stop her pain. She could have stripped naked in front of him right now, and he probably wouldn't have even noticed.

Correction. He'd notice. But he wouldn't care.

He unlocked the treatment cabinet, finding

a pair of surgical scissors. Carefully, gently, he cut the sleeve of her T-shirt, peeling the fabric back.

'Yeah, I think it is a partial dislocation.' Robbie was craning around, trying to see her shoulder, and he suppressed a smile. He'd probably be doing the same in her place.

'What's this?' He pointed to the small patch of what looked like eczema on her arm.

'You don't recognise eczema when you see it? I may be beginning to lose confidence in you.' There was a trace of weariness in her tone, as if she was used to these kinds of questions.

'I was going to fetch one of the nurses, to help you into a gown. But I'm thinking that you might prefer not to wear anything that's been washed in an unknown detergent.'

Suddenly there was warmth in her eyes. And with it came more tears. Robbie was battling to hold everything together and somehow he'd made her feel safe enough to let her guard down.

'You're right, I would prefer to stick with my own T-shirt.' She managed a smile. 'What's left of it.'

That smile was everything. Joel resisted the impulse to hug her, but couldn't help reaching out to lay a comforting hand on her left arm.

'Would you like something for the pain? Entonox?'

'I might save that for later.' Robbie knew what was coming just as well as he did. 'I'll scream if I want something.'

'You do that. Sit tight, I'll be a couple of minutes with the paperwork and then I'll take you for the X-ray.'

'You don't need—'

Joel turned away, ignoring Robbie's protest. He had no other patients to attend to and he really *did* need to make sure that she wasn't alone.

It had taken all of her single-minded stubbornness to get this far. As she'd turned into the quieter side entrance to the hospital, slowing to make sure that there was no traffic coming the other way on the slip road, someone had come out of nowhere hitting the back of the bike and sending her flying. The bike had ended up on a strip of grass beside the entrance to the hospital, and Robbie had ended up in agony.

But she'd got to her feet. That was the first step. The second step was get to her bike, and the third to get the pannier open and retrieve her courier bag, the pain in her shoulder rendering her right arm useless. She'd hardly noticed the car backing and driving away, leaving her alone, because single-mindedness didn't take account of anyone else's actions. She'd called Glen and then allowed herself to cry out from the pain, because there was no one to hear her. Then the fourth step. It had seemed like a very long way to the entrance of the A & E department, but the only way she was going to get there was to start walking.

And then Joel had found her. She'd almost wept with relief when she'd caught sight of him, trembling as he'd gently relieved her of the bag, and along with it all of the responsibility for taking the next step.

He hadn't pushed things, or tried to be the only doctor in the room. But he'd taken charge, and as Robbie had slowly begun to let go it had been difficult to hold back the tears.

His touch, his scent had been intoxicating enough to take the edge off the pain. And his matter-of-fact attitude to the patch of eczema he'd seen, and practical consideration, had stabbed even deeper. Now that she was alone, she could wallow in the luxury of embarrassment, knowing that Joel was dealing with everything else.

Right now, that embarrassment centred around her T-shirt. Even thinking about pulling it off made her feel slightly dizzy, and the X-ray required any metal to be removed from her clothing. She supposed she could call a nurse, but dealing with this herself, while Joel was out of the room, seemed a better option.

He'd left the scissors on the top of the treatment cabinet, and she reached for them. Using them to snip the bra strap that ran over her left shoulder was a bit awkward but easy enough, even if it did send pain thrumming through her. The right hurt even more, but it meant that she could now unhook her bra and pull it off without having to pull her T-shirt over her head.

The scissors slipped from her lap onto the floor, and she closed her eyes, breathing through the pain. Then she heard a soft rap on the door, and Joel entered, carrying a set of A & E treatment notes, and a temporary sling for her arm. He looked down at the pair of scissors, picking them up, and he must have been able to see the ruined bra that she was still clutching. Robbie felt herself redden.

'You decided not to wait for the nurse.' He grinned suddenly. 'I thought there was a secret trick to taking your underwear off under your clothes.'

Robbie couldn't help laughing. And every time Joel's warm humour touched her, making her feel safe and secure, she started to cry as well.

'If I told you, it wouldn't be a secret, would it? You need two working shoulders.' Her nose was beginning to run again and she snuffled awkwardly. Joel reached for a tissue, putting it into her hand.

'Too bad. This should make you a bit more comfortable until we get the X-ray results.'

He fixed the temporary sling, and then held her hoodie out so she could put her left arm into the sleeve before wrapping it around her shoulders. The trip down to the X-ray department was made with the minimum of fuss and since there wasn't a queue they didn't have to wait.

Joel spent a moment examining the results on the computer screen in the corner of the cubicle, and then turned to her. 'You want to take a look?'

'Of course.'

He twisted the screen around to face her. Robbie had expected to be able to give an informed and objective opinion about what should happen next, but somehow she couldn't. She stared dumbly at the image.

'This is what I think…' Joel was gently taking charge again, seeming to know that she couldn't. 'You've got a partial anterior dislocation, and it should reduce without too much trouble. You'll be having pain relief because it's going to hurt, and I'd like to do that now if it's okay with you.'

'Yes… Yes.' He was absolutely right, and had put it all into words when she couldn't.

'Right. You said Entonox? I can give you something a little stronger than that if you want.'

'Entonox is fine.' Robbie just wanted to get this over with.

'All right. We'll have this sorted very soon.' He gave her an encouraging smile, leaving the cubicle for a moment and then returning to help her out of her hoodie and the sling, gently supporting her as she lay back onto the bed. Kat, one of the nurses, appeared, bringing with her a bright smile and the cylinder of Entonox, and Joel handed her the mouthpiece.

He positioned himself on her left side. Close. No closer than he needed to be to do this, but it *was* close. She could feel his fingers on her shoulder and around her elbow. Maybe she should have asked for someone else to do this.

'Deep breath.' He nodded at the mouthpiece and Robbie sucked in a breath, feeling her head swim a little from the Entonox. 'Try to relax.'

That wasn't easy. Not when he was so close and she knew exactly what was coming. It clearly wasn't happening, because Joel hadn't pushed the shoulder joint back in yet.

'That's the trouble with doctors.' He grinned at Kat. 'They know what's going to happen next.'

'Nurses too.' Kat returned his smile.

'Yeah, nurses are the worst,' he joked, turning his head back towards Robbie. 'I'd say that this is going to hurt me more than it hurts you but...you can imagine it will if it makes you feel any better. Another breath.'

Suddenly she was floating in the languorous pool of his gaze. The floating part might well be the Entonox, but the warmth and the feeling of well-being were all down to Joel. She hardly registered his fingers tightening around her elbow, or the sharp pain that accompanied his swift, precise movement of her arm.

'Great. Well done.' His smile was everything. Robbie dropped the mouthpiece, almost reaching out for him before Kat put it back into her hand, encouraging her to take another breath.

Don't show yourself up now by clinging to him. Someone will say something and it'll be halfway around the hospital before you know it.

She struggled for self-control and found it, somewhere in his cool, professional touch. Something in Joel's eyes betrayed that hurting her *had* hurt him, and she hung onto that.

One small way that she could take control and be the one to offer comfort. She smiled up at him and he nodded.

'One more X-ray, just to make sure everything's back in the right place, and I'll sort out a sling for you. Then you can go home.'

CHAPTER THREE

JOEL HAD BEEN determined that Robbie should have the best. And he'd failed. Because the best involved a doctor who could step back and treat his patient with both care and objectivity. He'd managed the care part, but fallen down badly on the objectivity, although he'd managed to hide that. Robbie's case had been a simple one, and there had never been any doubt about the correct way to proceed.

A & E wasn't busy, and he handed the responsibility for helping Robbie back into her clothes and fitting her with a sling over to Kat, the nurse who had helped with the reduction. She raised her eyebrows when he asked her to reiterate the need for rest and keeping her shoulder immobile for at least three days, but Kat obviously knew Robbie.

'Leave the really tough jobs to the nurses, eh?'

Then everything became easier. While he

was waiting in the pharmacy queue for the painkillers he'd prescribed, he called Glen. He changed out of his scrubs on the way back, and by the time he arrived back in A & E he could slot effortlessly into the role of concerned friend, which allowed him a little more lassitude than the role of doctor.

She was sitting in the waiting room, her jacket on the chair next to her. Joel sat down on the adjoining seat, glad of the opportunity to keep a little space between them, because he just wanted to hug her.

'How's it feeling?'

'Much better, thanks.'

'Anything else you want to bring to our notice, before you go?'

She rolled her eyes. 'You gave me a thorough examination when I first got here. And Kat interrogated me just now, in case there was anything you'd missed.'

'Glad to hear it.' Joel leaned back in his seat, shooting her an innocent look. 'Did she manage to get anything out of you?'

'Just that I fell on my hip as well, and I think I may have a bruise tomorrow. And no, you're *not* going to take me back in there, because I showed it to Kat and it's just a bruise, which will be fine. I want to go home.'

Joel nodded. 'I spoke to Glen. They've collected your bike and it's back at the Tin Tabernacle. He says it's a bit scratched up but it doesn't look to be too badly damaged. He said you'd want to know.'

'I do, thanks. Not that I'll be riding it for a while.'

'No, not that you will. I told Glen that I'd take you home.'

Robbie narrowed her eyes. 'Thanks, but there's no need.'

'He seemed to think there was.' It was a convenient excuse, but not the whole truth. Joel had already decided that Robbie wasn't going home alone. 'There's always the option of reporting back and having Glen come down here, if you prefer that...'

Robbie shook her head, wincing slightly at the sudden movement. 'Don't do that. He'll be wanting to get home and have breakfast with Carla and the kids. And I wouldn't mind a helping hand if that's okay. I only seem to have one.'

Joel reckoned that this was about as close as he was going to get to an admission that she could do with some assistance. He respected her bravery and her independent spirit, even if it had wrenched at his heart to see her hurt and yet still putting the delivery she'd come to make first.

'By the way. I phoned up to the special care baby unit. They got your delivery and the baby's doing well.'

For a moment the news cut through her obvious fatigue. 'Thanks. I appreciate that.'

'And the taxi will be here in five minutes.'

She chuckled lazily, leaning back in her seat and closing her eyes. 'You're endlessly capable, aren't you…?'

Robbie leaned on him as they walked out to the taxi and let him help her inside. That was enough to allow Joel to step back a bit from any enjoyment he might have in being close to her, because you just didn't feel that with a friend in need. He had to prompt her for the address, and remind her to shift over to the left-hand side of the back seat, so that he could pass the seat belt over her uninjured shoulder.

The taxi slowed, driving around a quiet tree-lined square, the driver looking for the building number. Then it stopped outside a large mansion house, one of the solid stone facades that Joel generally only ever saw the outside of. He wondered whether there was some mistake, but then he saw Robbie release her seat belt. She tried reaching for her jacket, which lay beside her on the seat, puffing out a frustrated breath when Joel leaned forward to pay the driver.

He grabbed her jacket and helped her out of the vehicle. Robbie walked slowly towards the stone steps outside the building, and he followed her.

'Keys are in the top inside pocket of my jacket.'

Joel unzipped the pocket, handing her the keys, and she promptly dropped them. Robbie was clearly far too weary to do anything remotely practical, and he picked the keys up, trying a few in the lock of the heavy wooden door until he got the right one. Inside, was a lobby, with golden wood panelling on the walls and an air of understated wealth.

He wouldn't have been much surprised if Robbie had lived in some quirky, out of the way place, but this was *not* what he'd expected. She seemed at home here though, letting out a breath of relief when he closed the door behind them. She walked over to the lift, which opened immediately when she pressed the call button and revealed more glowing wood panelling.

'Top floor… You'll need the key…' She leaned against the back of the lift car, closing her eyes. Suddenly all that Joel could see was that she was in pain and couldn't wait to get home. He found the key that fitted the lock beside the button for the sixth floor, and when he twisted it the elevator started to move. When the lift doors opened they revealed just one front door and Joel sorted through the keys again to open it.

Then he saw nothing. Just Robbie's fatigue and her pain. He ushered her inside, and she walked into a large, light-filled sitting room and sat down on the sofa. Joel tried a few doors, finding the kitchen, and got a glass of water for her, opening the box of painkillers and handing her a couple.

She smiled at him wanly. 'Thanks. Sorry...'

'Don't you dare apologise. Take the painkillers, you obviously need them.'

'Yeah, I think I do.'

She put the tablets into her mouth and Joel handed her the glass of water to wash them down. Then he carefully arranged the cushions from the sofa, putting one at her back and another to support her arm in the right position.

'Thanks. Would you like some coffee or something...?'

Joel had been feeling a little like an intruder here, but Robbie obviously wanted him to stay. That was enough to stop him from walking away.

'I'll make it. Or would you prefer tea?'

She nodded. 'I was hoping you might offer. Coffee's good, I think I need to wake up a bit before I can get to sleep.'

He knew that feeling. The exhausted buzz after a busy night that made sleep impossible. She needed to eat something and get comfortable before she'd be able to rest properly.

'Can I get you something to eat?'

'There are some chocolate bars in the fridge. Take whatever you want for yourself.'

Sure. Chocolate and coffee might be a quick fix and about as far as Robbie could think at the moment. Good food and a warm drink would help her sleep a little better. She was shifting her feet restlessly, and she leaned forward to tug at the laces of her boots, wincing in pain as she did so.

He knelt down, unlacing her boots, and she didn't protest. Then Joel pulled a footrest over, propping her feet up on it and arranging a chunky knitted throw, which was slung over the armrest of the sofa, over her legs.

'Stay there. I'll get you something to eat.' It was gratifying that she hadn't put up even a murmur of protest.

'And coffee…'

'As long as I can work out how to operate your coffee machine.' Robbie's kitchen was smart and gleaming, and he'd noticed a coffee machine that looked as if you needed a two-day induction course before you even switched it on.

'Just pull levers…' She waved her hand, lazily. 'You'll be fine.'

He found a carton of soup in the fridge and heated it up, choosing a large mug from the kitchen cabinet that would be easy for her to manage one-handed. The coffee machine wasn't as complex as it looked, and there was some decaffeinated coffee in the cupboard, along with bread for toast. Joel added some fruit to the tray, and took it all through to the sitting room.

The analgesics had clearly kicked in, and she seemed more comfortable and alert, her cheeks a little less pale. She accepted the food gratefully, and Joel went back to the kitchen to fetch an ice pack from the freezer for her hip. He re-plumped the cushions at her back, just for good measure and because he wanted the gratification of being close to her. Then he sat, watching her drink the soup, as if his life depended on it.

'That's better.' She leaned forward to put her empty cup back onto the tray, and Joel took it from her before she had to stretch.

'You think you could get some sleep now?' He handed her the coffee.

'Maybe this will wake me up enough to move.' She took a sip and then another, as if she was making sure. 'It's decaf, isn't it...?'

He chuckled. 'I thought I was going to get away with that.'

'You can't fool me. When you work with kids you get a whole arsenal of little doctor tricks. You're dealing with an expert.'

Was that what it was? Little doctor tricks? Or little friend tricks? Or just the actions of someone who cared, but who couldn't bring himself to admit it.

'That shoulder's going to be pretty painful for a few days. But you should try to get some rest.'

She nodded. 'It's not too bad. Just as long as I don't do anything drastic like breathing. I feel as if I could just stay here and doze...'

That wasn't going to help much. It occurred to Joel that Robbie's eczema might make her going-to-bed routine more lengthy than just finding her bedroom and taking off her clothes, which was enough of a challenge at the moment.

'Can't face the emollients?' He said the words cautiously. The last time he'd mentioned her eczema she'd reacted as if it was a sore point.

'Something like that. I'm...um...sorry. That

I snapped at you when you asked about my eczema. You had a good point about the hospital gown and I wasn't thinking straight at the time.'

It had been one of the things he'd done right. Looking at her as a doctor who could see each of the things that might affect her medically. Forgetting that, as a man, all he could see was Robbie's hard-won smile.

Joel shrugged. 'It's okay. People have done a lot worse. I reckon that anyone who doesn't take a swing at me is a model patient.' Robbie could have done that if it would make her feel better. It probably would have made *him* feel better. The one thing that had been eating at him was her quiet vulnerability, and knowing that she was in a lot of pain.

'You have very low standards. I keep going until I get a smile.'

He'd bet she did. And he reckoned that in most cases she got one as well. He'd seen a new side of Robbie in the last few hours. Determination, certainly, but also patience and the willingness to make the best of things. She'd demanded nothing from him, and that had taken grit.

'You get a lot of that kind of thing? Comments about the eczema?' Joel always worked hard not to assume anything about anyone, but from Robbie's attitude he reckoned she did.

'That's one of the reasons I work with kids. They just ask what that funny red patch is and I tell them and they go *Oh, okay* and move on. Adults can be less forgiving.'

'You need to be *forgiven*?' Joel shot her a pained look and Robbie laughed.

'Me? No. It just makes me a bit weary when people say *Can't you cover it up with something?*' She stared up at the ceiling, as if wanting to avoid his gaze. 'Or that I must be able to afford some proper treatment…'

There was hurt, there. Joel suspected that she wasn't really talking about *people*, but one person in particular. Someone close… He felt himself shying away from the inevitable question, because whatever his remit was, it was definitely outside it.

'As if NHS doctors aren't as good as private doctors.' The attitude always made him frown.

'Yes, something like that. People have a habit of measuring things by how much they have to pay for them.' She turned her gaze on him as if something had just occurred to her. 'You're wondering how I afford this place on a doctor's salary?'

It would be an obvious lie to say no. The simple equation of square footage and location made the large room they were sitting in way beyond his own pay grade, and no doubt Robbie's as well. And it was nice square footage. High ceilings with moulded plasterwork, painted in different shades of cream that emphasised light and space. The furniture was plain but attractive and clearly of good quality. The one thing that wasn't understated was the light that hung from the centre of the ceiling. A huge globe, made up of swirling glass filaments, that fitted the proportions of the space, and gave it focus.

'It occurred to me. I reckon maybe a lottery win?'

She laughed suddenly. 'No. Ice-cold.'

'Rich uncle?'

'You're getting warmer... This was my grandparents' place. My grandfather died when I was nineteen and left it to me.'

She seemed almost apologetic. As if she was going through all the things that people had made her apologise for over the years, her eczema, her beautiful home, and challenging him with them. The thought that Robbie even cared about what he thought sent a tingle down his spine.

'I'll bet it's great for parties.'

Right answer. Robbie smiled suddenly. 'Yes,

it is. Thick walls so you can make as much noise as you like.'

And the whole of the top floor of the building, if the single front door outside the lift had been anything to go by. Joel wondered how many other large rooms there were, which he hadn't seen. Right now, the only one he was really interested in was Robbie's bedroom. He shivered at the thought, and adjusted his focus. Her bedroom with Robbie in it and fast asleep, and him somewhere else.

'If you need some help…getting ready for bed…' He felt himself flush and wondered what the professional way to say this might be. 'You've taken a nasty fall, and you're probably still a bit shaky. The last thing you need to do is fall again.'

Her gaze softened. 'You've already done too much, and I'm grateful. You must be tired.'

Nope. Wide awake. 'While I'm here, I may as well make myself useful.'

What was she doing? Testing him, that was what.

Robbie didn't much care what other people said, about anything in her life. Everyone thought what they thought, and as long as they didn't shove their opinions in her face she was happy to let them do that. She'd worked that out with her counsellor when she was a teenager.

Her parents could have sat back and enjoyed their wealth but instead they'd used it, not just sponsoring a variety of medical initiatives, but becoming personally involved with them as well. And wherever they went they took their daughters. She and her big sister, Izzy, had grown up in a world where everyone was taken just as they were, and if Robbie ever gave her eczema a second thought it was to realise that she faced fewer challenges than some of the other kids she knew.

And then suddenly, she'd become aware of it. A newspaper had published a photograph of her family, and drawn attention to the marks on her skin. The two most noticeable patches on her arm and face had even been enlarged in separate images, so that readers could examine them in detail. As if that were the only thing that mattered about her. Some journalist who didn't know her father from Adam had insinuated that it was Robbie's eczema that had prompted him to devote so much time and money to helping other kids.

It wasn't true. But Robbie had suddenly seen only Izzy's perfect skin and the marks on hers. She'd locked herself in her room, refusing to come out.

The matter had been dealt with, in the same way that her parents dealt with everything else that pertained to her and Izzy. Common sense and love. But even though Robbie had learned to appreciate her own worth and feel happy in her skin again, she hadn't quite managed to forget. Her parents had respected her decision to take a step back from the uncomfortable glare of the public eye, asking only that Robbie found her own ways of making a difference.

Then Rory. Dad had never liked him, and Robbie hadn't understood why. He'd seemed a little over-concerned about her eczema, but Robbie could cover it up if that was what he wanted. She'd just never been taught that there was a need to.

But Rory was the kind of person who couldn't feel truly happy if he wasn't better than everyone else. Robbie's trust fund suited him down to the ground on that score, and his attitude to her eczema was his way of making her feel unacceptable to anyone else. He'd chipped away at her confidence, until there was nothing left.

Finally she'd cracked. She'd realised how worthless Rory made her feel, and gone away on holiday without him, to give herself a chance to think.

When she'd returned she was ready to end

the relationship with Rory and to hear her father's thoughtful advice. *'Be whoever you want to be, Robbie. Money's only a burden if you allow it to be.'*

So Olivia Roberta Hampton-Hall had adopted the nickname her family had used for her since she was a child, and truncated her instantly recognisable surname, to become Robbie Hall.

All of her colleagues at the hospital and everyone at Nightshifters knew her as that. And it was her safe place, her refuge from the fear that some people would only ever see two things about her. Money and eczema.

Joel had seen both the money and the eczema, even though he didn't know it. Didn't know that her family's money was the reason Nightshifters existed. Regardless, neither had seemed to change the way he acted towards her. Why hide any more?

Because guarding those secrets was what made her feel safe and in control of her life. Loving someone like Joel would be horribly easy, someone who saw the things she kept hidden, but it stripped away everything that made her feel secure.

She was aware that she'd been silent for a while now. He hadn't pushed her, gathering the mugs and plates up, and taking them into the kitchen. From the sounds of it, he was doing the washing up. Robbie put her mind to how she was going to reach the fading eczema patches from her last flare, and even thinking about it made her shoulder hurt. And Joel was here and he'd offered his help.

Robbie swallowed her last gulp of coffee and with it a slice of her hard-won self-reliance.

When he reappeared from the kitchen, she said, 'I think I need some help. If you don't mind.'

He smiled, shaking his head. 'Of course not. What do you need?'

Joel had followed her to her bedroom, stopping abruptly at the door, until she beckoned him in. He'd opened the wide drawers, which wouldn't budge if she tugged at just one of the handles, and she'd found a soft, comfortable nightshirt, which had the added advantage of having long sleeves and reaching down to her knees.

Then came the awkward part. But Joel was well practised in making the very awkward seem hardly difficult at all, sitting her down on the bed and then unclipping the sling and laying her arm on a pillow that he'd placed on her lap. Then he spread the nightshirt out next to her on the bed and drew back.

'Undress your uninjured side first...' He'd

retreated back through the open doorway and was out of sight now, but from the sound of his voice Joel was standing right outside in the hall. And clearly attempting to be of some use from a distance.

'I know.'

Getting out of the T-shirt and threading the part of it that Joel had cut away at the hospital over her injured shoulder was easy enough. The nightshirt was a bit more tricky, but she managed to get the sleeve over her right shoulder without too much pain.

'It sounds easier than it actually is.'

She heard his low chuckle. 'I've never tried it. Are you okay?'

'Just about.' She'd forgotten to undo the buttons at the neck of the nightshirt, and it was stuck over her head.

'Do you need a hand? I could keep my eyes closed…'

Robbie gave the nightshirt a tug and felt it give. The button had flown off and clattered against something. That was okay, she'd find it later. She could get her left arm through the sleeve of the loose garment now.

'How are you going to help with your eyes closed? You wouldn't be able to even find me, you'd have to feel your way.'

His embarrassed cough made her smile. And

then the incongruity of the situation struck her, and she started to laugh. Two doctors being shy with each other over getting into a night-shirt. Really?

Pain shot through her shoulder, making her yelp and bringing tears to her eyes. Then she felt Joel, his arms around her, gently support-ing her shoulder. She clutched at his shirt, burying her head against his chest.

'Just breathe. You're okay.'

Yeah. Breathe. That was what she'd forgot-ten to do. The first breath made her whimper with pain but the second one wasn't so bad. The third was positively delicious, as she took in his warm, clean scent.

'Better?'

'Yes.' Great actually, despite the throbbing in her shoulder. 'I didn't knock it back out again, did I?'

She felt his fingers on her shoulder, so gentle that his probing didn't even hurt. 'No, you'd know if you did and it feels fine. This is the *It's going to be painful for a while* part.'

'I might say that with a bit more emphasis in future, when I'm dealing with patients.'

'Being a patient is generally a much tougher job than being a doctor.' He drew back and Robbie glimpsed tenderness in his eyes, be-fore he turned his attention to the sling, carefully putting it back on to support her shoulder again.

That was what marked Joel out. He wasn't just kind, he'd been there for her in a way that was both touching and supportive. He probably didn't take all of his patients home and make soup for them, but Robbie wouldn't blame any of them for being a little in love with him.

He helped her out of her jeans, his deft fingers not once touching her skin, although she wouldn't have minded if they had. Then he fetched the emollients and cleansing creams from her bathroom, laying them out on the bed so she could choose which ones she wanted.

'These two will do for now.' She'd work out a way to continue her usual moisturising routine later.

'Hands, knees and elbows?' He grinned. It clearly wasn't lost on him that, while they were the usual trouble areas for eczema, they were also relatively safe territory.

'Yes, that's good. I have a small patch on my left shoulder that I can't reach, and the one you saw just above my right elbow.' In the warmth of his smile, elbows were taking on a major sexual significance that she'd never considered before.

'Sounds good. I'll just go and wash my hands with your soap if that's okay...'

He missed nothing. And he seemed to find that gentle rhythm that Robbie used when she cleaned and moisturised her skin, not stressed and resentful but using this as an opportunity for leisurely self-care. It would—should—have been relaxing, but her nerve ends were tingling at his every touch.

'Just as well you're left-handed.' His observation was clearly intended to be the kind of conversation that would put her at her ease, but it didn't. Joel had been noticing things about her.

'Yeah, I guess so. I never realised quite how much I use my right hand though.'

He nodded. 'Are you ready to sleep?'

She could spend all day just talking to Joel. But he looked tired and Robbie had to admit she was feeling sleepy now too. A picture of lying down to sleep, curled up in his arms, floated into her head.

It would be safe and secure. Robbie added to the picture in her head—a couple of layers of clothing and bedding between them—but that made it only slightly less delicious. It was still far too good to be a practical possibility.

Maybe she'd wake up in the morning and feel better. She'd wonder why it had ever seemed so necessary to cling to him.

Joel seemed undeterred by her silence. He

was plumping pillows and arranging them so that she could sit up comfortably in the bed, and then he drew the duvet back. He seemed to have everything in hand and Robbie went with the flow.

But he was steadily getting ready to leave. When he went to fetch her phone from the sitting room, putting it in reach beside the bed, Robbie made one last effort to make him stay, shifting herself upright on the pillows.

'Don't close the curtains. Not yet...'

He took the hint, pulling the comfortable wicker chair from the corner and sitting down, stretching his long legs out in front of him.

'How did I do? In terms of interesting cases, tonight.' *This* was something they could talk about. Something that they had in common that didn't allow for any thoughts of how it might feel to have him touch her.

Joel grinned lazily. 'Well...good marks for accurate self-diagnosis, before you even arrived. But unfortunately you don't get the top prize for the night. That goes to Edna.'

'I'm mortified. Who's Edna?'

'She's an elderly lady who came in at about two in the morning. She'd fallen and couldn't get back up again, and pressed her personal alarm. When the ambulance brought her in she was wearing her nightie and dressing gown, with a hat. Apparently she'd insisted that the paramedic fetched her hat for her, before she'd agree to come to the hospital with them.'

'I knew I'd forgotten something.' Robbie smiled. Talking about the routine of other people's ailments was surprisingly relaxing. 'Was she okay…?'

CHAPTER FOUR

ROBBIE WOKE AT five in the afternoon. Her shoulder was throbbing, an acute reminder of the feeling of panic as she'd parted company with her bike and felt herself hit the ground. Her hip was stiff and sore as well.

Then she remembered. The relief when Joel had found her. X-rays, soup and then hearing about Joel's night at work, which had made a world that seemed to be spinning out of control more reassuringly normal. She'd started to doze halfway through his story about a practical joke that one of the nurses had played, and Joel had rearranged the pillows so that she could lie down.

Everything was in its proper place, the curtains were closed and the wicker chair he'd been sitting in back in the corner of the room. Had he gone? Her bedroom door was open and she listened carefully. Silence. Of course he'd left.

A dangerous thought entered her mind. A thought she shouldn't give space. She wanted him back. Robbie felt alone and vulnerable, and…she just wanted Joel back. Maybe a good cry would help, but that wasn't her usual modus operandi. She'd feel better if she found something to occupy her.

She got out of bed carefully, wrapping her dressing gown around her without bothering to go through the rigmarole of removing the sling to put her right arm into the sleeve. Knotting the tie was a problem and she left the gown open, walking towards the kitchen. Hopefully Joel had left her analgesics somewhere she could find them.

Then she saw that the sitting-room door was wide open and the blinds were closed, light filtering through them. She padded into the room and found Joel, stretched out on the sofa under the knitted throw, and fast asleep. Just the sight of him was enough to realise that the doctor-patient gratitude effect hadn't worn off yet. He still looked just as sexy and she could watch him sleep for any amount of time.

The temptation to give in to tears of gratitude was indescribable. He'd stayed, and he was obviously tired because the sound of her moving around hadn't woken him. She'd let him sleep a little while longer, secure in the knowledge that he was still here.

Robbie crept into the kitchen, opening the fridge and taking out a bottle of water. Getting the tablets out of the foil pack was a little awkward, but easy enough once she worked out how, and she laid them on the worktop next to the sink. The bottle was a greater challenge, the top stubbornly refusing to turn. Maybe if she ran it under some cold water...

The bottle slipped in her wet fingers and smashed into the sink. Great. And to add to her helpless frustration, she heard a noise from the sitting room and then Joel appeared at the kitchen door, obviously wide awake now.

'Sorry. I was going to let you sleep.'

'Are you all right?' His gaze took in the broken remains of the bottle. 'Did you cut yourself?'

'I dropped it. I'm...' Right now, nothing else mattered, apart from the fact that he was here. 'You stayed.'

'Yeah. You muttered something about a spare room as you were going to sleep, so I reckoned it would be okay with you.' He shrugged, turning the corners of his mouth down.

'It's fine. I really appreciate that you did. I wish you'd taken the spare room—you would have been more comfortable.' His feet were bare but he was still wearing his jeans and shirt, and his hair was sticking out a little. Perfect. Gorgeous.

'The sofa was fine. I reckoned I'd be able to hear you if you got up, but...'

'You were tired. I'm sorry I woke you. And I really appreciate all you did to help me this morning.'

He grinned suddenly, running his hand through his hair to flatten it. It was a great morning look. 'My pleasure. Leave the glass, I'll clear it up. Do you want something to eat?'

'Coffee would be great. With caffeine this time.' Robbie went to the fridge, taking out a fresh bottle of water, and Joel took it from her, opening it. She collected her tablets from the worktop, and sat down at the kitchen table. If she was going to have to submit to being looked after for a little while longer then she might as well enjoy it.

Watching him was *very* enjoyable, and when his back was turned she could do it as brazenly as she liked. Broad shoulders that gave the appearance of muscle when he stretched. Slim hips emphasised by a pair of jeans that looked as if they'd been washed a hundred times, because they fitted in all the right places. She must have been in a bad way when they'd arrived back here this morning, because she hadn't even noticed that.

And he had the best waking-up smile she'd ever seen. A little lazy, with the suggestion that dreams weren't just things that happened when you were asleep. Her immobilised shoulder suddenly became a *lot* more frustrating, because there was nothing she could do in response except smile back.

If he'd had to wrestle with the coffee machine the first time around, he had it under control now. He put her coffee down in front of her and sat down.

'I should be getting going soon, if I'm going to be at the Tin Tabernacle this evening. Is there anything you need?'

Robbie took a deep breath. This couldn't go on; she had to stand on her own two feet. The longer he stayed, the more difficult it would be to let him go, and not letting a guy go wasn't anywhere on her agenda.

'There's nothing I need, thank you.' She gave him a smile. 'I really appreciate all that you've done, but it's time for me to chase you away.' Robbie phrased it as tactfully as she could. What she really meant was that it was time for her to stop ogling him.

He gave her a thoughtful look. 'You can manage?'

Right now she felt that all she really needed was Joel's smile. That was the best reason of all for sending him away.

'I can manage. This is what happens after we decide that patients don't need to be taken in to the hospital and send them home to get some rest.'

Joel nodded. 'And that's what you're planning on doing?'

Good question. 'I'd prefer to be at the Tin Tabernacle tonight, and back at work on Sunday night.' She saw a flash of alarm in his eyes. 'I'm telling myself right now that's not going to happen.'

'No, it isn't. At the very least you should be staying home until you've seen someone in Orthopaedics for a follow-up appointment—' He broke off suddenly as Robbie shot him a querying look. 'You remember that?'

'Uh…yes, you did say something about it last night, didn't you?'

Robbie wasn't sure that the follow-up appointment was strictly necessary. She was a doctor and she knew what she should do to care for her shoulder. But, on the other hand, it wasn't very likely that she'd be allowed back to work without an all-clear from Orthopaedics.

'Are you working up a list of reasons why you don't need to see a specialist?' He seemed to be able to read her mind without any effort at all.

'I was thinking it through. If my reasons are looking a bit flimsy to me, I imagine you'll be able to knock them over in no time.'

He nodded, amusement showing in his face. 'You might be overestimating me.'

Robbie doubted it. But the idea of putting up a fight, and seeing who got the better of whom, was much too tempting at the moment. She got to her feet, trying to shake off the delicious feeling that when she was with Joel she was somewhere warm and comfortable, that she didn't want to leave.

It was just doctor-patient infatuation kicking in again. He was a good doctor and he was easy on the eye, and Robbie guessed that many of his patients developed symptoms.

'I can manage. And I'll do as I've been told, I promise.'

Robbie was concentrating on giving him no reason to stay. And Joel was clearly getting the message, because he got to his feet, draining his cup and walking through to the sitting room, to put on his socks and shoes.

'You've got my number?'

'Yes, you gave it to me last week.'

'Use it, then, if you need it.' He paused, waiting for her assent, and Robbie nodded.

She'd left him no reason to stay now. Robbie hovered at the front door while he called the lift, and then decided that gave all the wrong signals. She gave him a final, cheery goodbye and a thank-you and closed the door.

Leaning against it, she heard the lift doors open, and a slight creak as he stepped inside. She closed her eyes, trying hard not to cry. The apartment seemed suddenly very big and very empty, and the safest corner of it was right here, where she was closest to Joel.

'Stupid…' Robbie muttered a reproach, and tore herself away from the door. Joel had been here, he'd been kind, and now he was gone. That was exactly what she wanted, for him to take that perfect body of his somewhere it wouldn't wreak such havoc. The next time she saw him, he'd just be another volunteer, who didn't make her heart swell with longing.

An hour later, Robbie was still going through the process of getting showered and dressed in her head. It seemed like a great deal of trouble if she wasn't going to be going anywhere, and she was warm and comfortable on the sofa, wrapped in her thick dressing gown. Then the doorbell rang, and Rosie's voice floated over the intercom.

Rosie arrived, trailing the scent of a large

bunch of freesias behind her, and immediately started to rap out orders. Robbie wasn't to move, while she found a vase. She could indulge in a little light flower arranging, while Rosie made a cup of tea.

'Yes, ma'am.' Robbie grinned at Rosie, glad to have the everyday clatter of activity around her again.

'Don't be smart, Rob.' Rosie clearly had her nursing hat on at the moment. 'Glen said he'd be popping in and, you never know, he might bring something to eat. You need to keep your strength up.'

Glen arrived, with a kitchen container full of food, adding the scent of cooking to that of the flowers. Clearly there was a concerted effort to try and make the place smell like home. Rosie peeled open the lid.

'Oh. Chicken jerk.' Rosie grinned. 'Carla's mum's recipe?'

'Of course, what other recipe is there?' Glen replied. 'Leftovers from lunch, and there's more than enough for two.'

Clearly these weren't leftovers, and Carla had deliberately cooked a few extra portions. Rosie added her thanks to Robbie's and disappeared into the kitchen.

'How's it going?' Glen lowered himself onto the sofa next to her.

'Oh…you know.' Robbie puffed out a breath. 'It hurt, and then Joel administered a sharp crunch and it felt a bit better. I'll be fine in a week.'

'Bit more than a week, Rob.'

'Maybe. Maybe I'll stun you all with my amazing powers of recuperation.' Robbie had picked up her phone to text Carla and frowned at the screen. 'I've just told Carla Thank you for the goofs. Who knew that texting with one hand was so fiddly?'

'Give it here.' Glen held out his hand and Robbie dropped the phone into it. He typed *food* into another text and sent it.

'What time did you get home this morning?' Glen worked the day shift during the week and usually dropped in to the Tin Tabernacle at either the beginning or the end of the night, to check on how things were going.

'About half past ten. Just in time to take the kids to the park before they tore the house down.'

'Not before you made Joel come home with me.' Robbie injected a note of reproach into the words.

'He insisted, actually. Told me I didn't need to come because he was going to see you home and make sure you were all right.'

A tingle ran down Robbie's spine. Joel hadn't

mentioned it was his idea. What did that mean? Best not enquire any further.

'By the way, I got a little something for Amelia's birthday. Would you be able to take it now? I'm not sure whether I'll be able to come to her party next week—'

Glen shot her a warning look. 'Don't even try it, Rob. A dozen over-excited eight-year-olds don't mix well with a dislocated shoulder. If you want to come over, come to dinner another evening.'

'Thanks. You'll take the present, though—I'd like her to have it on her birthday. It's on the top shelf of the cupboard in the hall in a blue and white bag.'

Glen went to fetch it, and returned inspecting the contents of the bag, smiling at the roll of sparkly princess wrapping paper. 'Oh… This is the book she wanted.'

'I hope she likes it. Dad was at a thing, and he got it signed for her.'

Glen flipped open the cover, reading the author's message, wishing Amelia a happy birthday. 'She'll be over the moon with this. Thank David for me, won't you? Have you called your mum and dad?'

'Not yet. They were in Ireland all of last week and they're flying back tonight. I'll give

Mum a call in the morning, and no doubt she'll be all over it.'

'Good. So you want me to call the Night-shifters off your case?'

Robbie laughed. 'It means a lot that you came, I'm really grateful. But yes, please do call them off, I can only take so much looking after before I start climbing out of the window and shimmying down the drainpipe.' Hopefully that message would get through to Joel, as well.

'Not on my watch, you're not.' Rosie appeared with the tea and sat down, opening the roll of princess paper so that she could wrap Amelia's present.

It was nice, having her friends here. The comfortable, easy laughter and the good-natured bossiness. It took the edge off missing a man that she had no business missing.

And she and Joel were over. Finished, before they'd even started. It had seemed so real, and maybe he had felt it too, but it was a relationship that wasn't meant to happen. She wouldn't allow it to.

Joel had heard the messages. Glen had popped in, and was satisfied that Robbie was all right and not overdoing things. Rosie would be staying the night with her. After that, Robbie's mother would be coming to stay for a few days.

He wasn't needed. Robbie had made it clear that he wasn't wanted, even though she'd couched it in the nicest of terms—he'd done enough and she had to let him go. That suited him just fine, because he wasn't looking for a relationship with her. He knew himself too well, his relationships had a limited shelf-life and Robbie was the type of woman that deserved much more than something that fell apart of its own accord after a few weeks.

He had some thinking to do. Joel had seen Robbie at her most vulnerable, and he knew from experience that patients acted out of character when they were in shock and in pain. The idea that he should feel anything different from the cool professionalism that he usually brought with him to these encounters was a new one.

Waiting was hard, when he couldn't help wanting to see her. Couldn't help wondering whether she was all right, although he knew she was being well looked after. But he had to do it, because the dynamic between them was all wrong. He'd been a doctor and she'd been a patient, and that had opened up the prospect of all kinds of inappropriate feelings, the kind that they might regret later.

So he would wait. When Robbie was over the initial shock of what had happened, then maybe she would want to be his friend. And he'd be satisfied with that. He'd have to be.

CHAPTER FIVE

ROBBIE EMERGED FROM her consultation, clutching a handful of patient leaflets, her ears ringing. The head of orthopaedics didn't usually bother herself with a simple shoulder dislocation, but she was the firmest person that Robbie had ever met. She was beginning to wonder whether Orthopaedics weren't taking a leaf out of Nightshifters' and her parents' playbook and ganging up on her.

Then a ray of sunshine made her stop in her tracks, almost blinding her. Joel was sitting quietly at the back of the waiting room.

She could have been forgiven for not noticing him, and walking straight towards the exit. But her legs were already carrying her towards him, and she could feel herself smiling, with every inch of her body. Even her shoulder seemed to be doing its own version of smiling, and had stopped throbbing.

'Hey.' She sat down beside him. 'What are you doing here?'

The answer to that appeared to require some thought. 'Glen told me you had an appointment to come and see Dr Thompson.'

'You asked?' The thought that maybe he was here because he wanted to be, and not because Glen had hinted that he should be, was suddenly important.

Joel smiled. 'Yes. I asked. I wanted to see how you were.'

Five days of being without Joel had been enough time for Robbie to convince herself that what she'd felt for him really was just gratitude. It had taken about ten seconds for her to change her mind. Right now, she could think of a dozen different ways to inconvenience him, all of which felt perfectly acceptable.

'My parents came to stay for a few days. It was lovely to spend some time with Mum and Dad, but they've been looking after me to within an inch of my sanity. And now I've been subjected to a thorough talking to from the head of orthopaedics. You should bear Dr Thompson in mind for your more difficult patients—she's terrifying.'

'Yeah?' He raised an eyebrow. 'You don't look all that terrified...'

'That's because I'm annoyed.' Robbie frowned.

'Why? What did she say?' He pulled a face, seeming to regret his questions. 'Asking for a friend, you understand.'

It seemed that he was asking for himself. But Robbie understood why he wouldn't say so, because she was confused too. Caught in the middle of a battle between her instinctive feelings for Joel, and the way she'd planned her life.

'My friend?'

His eyes grew warmer and he nodded. 'Yes, your friend.'

They knew where they stood, now. And friendship could be any number of things, so there was a way forward for them both.

'She gave me exercises.' Robbie handed him the printed sheets and Joel glanced through them, nodding.

'Looks good.'

'They are, and she'll be giving me a rocket if she thinks I haven't done them every day. And she says that I can come back to work, which is good, but that she's going to call my head of department and discuss light duties with him. I've got to go back and have her sign me off before I can actually do my job.'

'Is there such a thing as light duties in A & E?'

Robbie turned the corners of her mouth

down. 'I wasn't aware of that either. I reckoned I'd be okay if I had a nurse with me to help, but apparently I'm not allowed to do that, I have to just talk to people. She says that I can answer their questions and give them general guidance, after they've seen the doctor.'

'Sounds like a great idea. I wish we had someone like that full time, I don't always have the time to go through everything as thoroughly as I'd like with patients.'

'It is a great idea. I just didn't want it to be me!'

He leaned back in his seat, a smile playing around his lips. 'Something tells me that you don't want to hear what I think.'

That was what she liked about Joel. They could disagree without it having to turn into an argument.

'Go on. Say it.'

'You think that Dr Thompson's not assessed you properly?'

'No, she's fierce but she's an incredibly good doctor.' Robbie had to admit that.

'Then… What you did on Saturday morning was incredibly brave. You were in shock from an accident, and a lot of pain, and somehow you managed to get up and collect your courier bag and walk.'

The thought of the effort that it had taken

still made her tremble. Robbie turned her head away from him, blinking away the tears that were forming in her eyes.

'Look at me.' His words were gentle, but Robbie responded angrily, glaring at him. The softness in his gaze only made her want to cry even more.

'You can stop now, Robbie. You did it, you made the delivery and you got yourself some help. You've said yourself that Dr Thompson is a good doctor, and you can let her take the strain, and dictate what pace you need to go at to recover properly. That's *her* job, not yours.'

Warmth. The sudden feeling of a weight being lifted. And the equal and opposite feeling that she could do this by herself.

'That's what you think, is it?'

His gaze didn't waver. 'Yeah, it is. You did what you had to do, and there are powerful emotions behind that. It's okay to still feel them, but you can make your decisions on a more rational level now.'

Somehow that sounded like a promise. One that Robbie wanted to make, because it seemed that Joel was making it too. What they felt for each other was too powerful to either dismiss or ignore.

'I'm not going to give you the satisfaction

of admitting you're right, Joel, even though you are.'

He chuckled, leaning back in his seat. 'I wouldn't expect any less from you.'

The bustle of the hospital, the familiar world around her, seemed to move back into focus. Normality was piecing itself back together again, and Joel was there, beckoning to her. Robbie could take his friendship and deal with the rest as it happened.

'How do you feel about breakfast?'

He smiled. 'Much the same as usual. I'm always up for breakfast whatever time my body clock's set to.'

'Me too. And I know just the place...'

Robbie directed him through a maze of backstreets, stopping at a small patisserie on the way. He guessed that her other 'job' with the Nightshifters had given her this encyclopaedic knowledge of every shortcut in the area, and he wasn't much surprised when he realised that they were heading for the Tin Tabernacle. He drew up in the small parking area behind the building, next to the two cars that the Nightshifters used, and switched off the engine.

'Couldn't keep away, eh?'

'This is a social call.' She opened the car door, managing to get out of the low seat without any help from him, and Joel grabbed the bag from the patisserie. Whatever was wrapped up inside smelled great, but Robbie seemed to have bought too much for two.

The towpath was deserted, and Robbie led him around to the front of the Tin Tabernacle, opening the door. Walking to the back of the space, she unlocked another door, set into the partition behind the desks.

'What the…?' Joel had thought this must be a small storeroom, but he'd miscalculated the footprint of the building. It was a good-sized area, shelved out and well organised. There was an impressive array of medical stores and equipment, along with handyman's tools and supplies, which he supposed were necessary to keep a building of this age and type in good condition.

Robbie grinned. 'Working at night, we need to be self-sufficient.' She pointed to a neat stack of folding chairs and tables. 'Would you bring these out for me, please? And take two chairs and a table and put them outside on the towpath.'

Joel decided to go with the flow. Having coffee here had seemed a little pointless, when it would be nicer to go to a café somewhere, but Robbie obviously had something else in mind. He did as she asked, moving the tables and chairs out of the storeroom, before Robbie closed the door again and locked it.

He took a couple of chairs outside, placing a table between them, and then went to find Robbie. She was wrestling with the coffee machine, but seemed to be managing, and he waited while she made two cups of coffee, then picked them up along with the patisserie bag and followed her back outside.

It was a little chilly, but she sat down, drawing her jacket around her. Joel took a couple of paper napkins from the bag, along with two of the pastries. They were still warm and he laid them down next to their coffee cups.

'This is nice…' He wasn't all that sure that it was, but Robbie seemed content with the arrangement. Maybe just being here was lifting her spirits, and he wasn't going to argue with that.

A wiry man with a grey beard and wearing a check jacket climbed out of a brightly painted boat moored a little way along the towpath. As he strolled towards them, Joel saw that he was holding a mug.

'Hi, Robbie. What have you gone and done to yourself?' He nodded towards the sling.

'*I* didn't do anything. Someone knocked me off my bike and dislocated my shoulder.'

'Ouch.' The man grimaced. 'I'll bet that hurt.'

'I was lucky, I happened to be turning into the hospital when it happened.' Robbie turned to Joel. 'Joel, this is Roy. He lives over there.'

Roy held out his hand and Joel shook it. 'You're with the Nightshifters? I saw you here the other day.'

'Yes, I've just started here.' Joel couldn't conceal his surprise. No one could miss the boats lining the towpath, but they were just a gaily painted backdrop and he'd walked past them without really considering who might be living in them.

Roy chuckled. 'No secrets around here.'

That wasn't a bad thing. Joel had lived his life trying to shed the burden of his father's secrets and he liked the idea of a place where everyone knew what everyone else was doing.

'Apart from the fact that we're even here?' Robbie chimed in. 'Not a lot of people know that.'

Roy nodded sagely. 'Yes. Apart from that.'

Discomfort trickled down Joel's spine. Maybe it was impossible to live entirely without some kind of secret. But Robbie was grinning up at Roy and he dismissed the thought.

'You know where the coffee machine is.'

'I do.' Roy didn't seem surprised about the offer and strolled round to the entrance of the Tin Tabernacle. A young couple were walking towards them now, and they were introduced as Chloe and Grant, here for the summer from Australia and due to fly home in a month's time. Chloe put the biscuit tin she was carrying down on the table, and followed Roy inside to make coffee, and Grant fetched more chairs and another table.

Joel understood now. People were appearing from the boats to join them, some bringing something with them, others just bringing themselves. Clara and Joan lived here because they liked the river and somehow managed to run a knitwear business from the confines of their narrowboat. Terry worked at the floating restaurant a little further along the towpath, and Kamal with a local theatre group. Roy was a writer, and when he went back to his boat to fetch one of his books for Joel, he realised that he was talking to the author of a string of bestsellers. Someone brought a chess set, and a small group gathered around one of the tables to watch and discuss each move that the players made.

The news of Robbie's accident had spread quickly, and each of the dozen people seated in groups around the tables had come up to her to ask how she was. Clara had gone back to her boat and reappeared with a brightly coloured knitted scarf for her, and she and Joan had insisted that she take it, wrapping it carefully around her shoulders. Joel reckoned that if anything would help heal her, this definitely would.

'This happens a lot?' Joel asked in one of the few moments that Robbie wasn't in conversation with someone.

'Most mornings. Whenever we're here we always open up the Tabernacle, but otherwise it'll be somewhere along the towpath, or on one of the boats in the winter.'

'How does everyone know where to go?'

Robbie chuckled. 'Everyone just knows. It's easy to think that you're alone here at night, but you never are. The Tin Tabernacle was first built here as a place for people working the barges that travelled up and down this stretch of water, and although that's changed we still try to play our part in the community. We hold two afternoon surgeries a week here. We'd like to do more but we can't get the volunteers.'

'I never would have thought…' Joel shook his head.

'Most people don't. They drive over the bridges, or walk along the towpath, and they just see boats. They don't realise that people are here, living their lives.'

'And you like being under the radar, like this?' The question was more important to him than just a way of passing the time, and it seemed to be more important to Robbie as well, because she considered it carefully.

'It's not something that anyone really goes out to do. But yes—that was one of the things that attracted me…' She paused, pressing her lips together as if she'd made a faux pas. 'It suits Nightshifters. Being tucked away here, so that we can get on with what we're aiming to do.'

'But everyone knows about the work that Nightshifters does.' Joel was struggling with the idea that he'd joined some kind of secret society that appeared every now and then to help when there was a crisis, then disappeared again.

She turned her gaze on him, and suddenly he felt he knew all he needed to know. 'Don't sweat it. We're here, and we are what we are.'

Robbie was right. He didn't need to examine everything so closely, wondering what it might conceal. They were talking about Nightshifters, nothing more.

'Everyone here seems to get along.'

'Not always. It's like living anywhere. There's always someone who'll play loud music all night or be a nuisance. But they tend to either mend their ways or move on, because it's hard living here if you don't have the support of the people around you.'

Joel had so many questions. They could wait, because Robbie was obviously thriving on the chatter around her, and anyway it appeared that a lot of things just happened of their own accord rather than being planned out. It was a bit like being a stranger in a small village, hidden away somewhere—the best thing to do was just listen and watch and the rules became obvious.

It seemed that one of those rules was that morning coffee lasted for a whole hour, but not much longer. The chess pieces were dropped back into their box, plates were cleared away and cups washed, and the tables and chairs were neatly stacked by the door of the storeroom. Everyone said their goodbyes, and meandered back to their boats, blending back in with the people who were toing and froing along the towpath.

'Thank you. I really enjoyed coming here.' Joel turned to her, smiling. 'Time to go home now?'

'Yep. If I'm going to be on time for work tonight, I'd better get some sleep.' Robbie hid a yawn behind her hand.

'Tonight?' Joel tried to control his pleasure at seeing Robbie again so soon.

'Yes, Dr Thompson said she'd speak to my head of department today, and work something out with him. She suggested I switch to working from Monday to Friday, instead of Sunday to Thursday as well.'

'Not a bad idea. Sunday nights can be busy. Would you like a lift into work? It's not much of a detour.'

Robbie laughed. 'I'm tempted to say that I can manage. But even thinking about a crowded Tube train makes me flinch at the moment.'

She was still fighting it. Still refusing to accept what she, as a doctor, should know better than anyone else. Joel had learned one thing this morning, though.

The way he cared about her wasn't just because she was hurt and vulnerable. That had just allowed him to open his heart to her, and when he had she'd swanned in, taking up residence there. He was beginning to wonder whether he wasn't in this for keeps, and, since he could no longer write this off as a passing attraction that would fade with time, he would have to call it a friendship. One that felt stronger and far more urgent than any friendship he'd ever had before.

So much for the theory of being a little in love with the man simply because he'd saved you.

Joel wasn't just that any more, and Robbie still had to grapple with the temptation to step a little closer to him. But they'd been important enough to each other to pull away from the doctor/patient dynamic and be friends. They could be important enough to each other to stay friends, and not cross the dangerous line into lovers.

Made all the more difficult because it had been decided that Robbie's new role was most needed in the main A & E unit. The pleasure of being able to see Joel as he walked back and forth, between patients, was mitigated by the impossibility of the task she'd been set. Sitting behind a desk, she had found herself with an unregulated queue of patients all wanting to get home. Joel had noticed the pressure she was under, trying to juggle the questions and the grumbles about having to wait yet *again*, and suggested an amendment to the plan. The A & E doctors should call her into the patient's cubicle when they were ready, which allowed her to deal with one patient at a time, and was a great deal less stressful.

And it was working. Glen had told her that if he saw her at the Tin Tabernacle this weekend he'd take her back home himself, but Joel had promised they'd go somewhere else to eat on Saturday morning. He hadn't said where they were going and Robbie hadn't asked; it somehow heightened the feeling of anticipation.

'I'm not going to ask, because I actually don't want you to tell me where we're going.' She got into his car, settling herself into the passenger seat.

'It's nowhere special…' He shrugged and Robbie held up one finger to silence him.

'I like surprises.'

'You do? I'll bear that in mind.'

Their route out into the suburbs of London was certainly a surprise. After half an hour they drew up outside a row of small two-up two-down cottages.

'Is this where you live?' He helped her out of the car and Robbie looked around her, unable to see any other reason for stopping here.

'Yep.'

Suddenly the whole street took on a new and rosier perspective. Particularly the house with wooden blinds at the windows and a green front door, which Joel was leading her towards.

She caught a glimpse of pale walls and lots of books through the door into the sitting room as he led her to a large room at the back. The back room and scullery had been knocked together and extended to make a large kitchen with a dining area. There were no frills, but Joel obviously liked the uneven quality of natural and traditional materials because they were everywhere. Seagrass matting on top of stripped floorboards, an original cast-iron stove, and what looked like reclaimed bricks for the patio outside.

'Outside or inside?'

She could see a couple of wicker chairs and a table outside on the patio, and the sun was enough to cut through a little of the morning's chill.

'Let's go outside.'

Robbie settled herself into one of the chairs. The small walled garden was low maintenance, with plants and shrubs in clay pots, but it was like a little oasis of calm. Joel joined her from the kitchen, a bottle and two glasses in one hand.

'I thought we might drink a toast. To how far you've come in the last week.' He put the bottle down on the table. 'It's alcohol free, but it does have bubbles.'

That was just as well, as she was still taking painkillers. 'Bubbles are the main thing.'

The cork came out with a satisfying pop, and Joel poured the drinks. Sitting down, he tipped his glass against hers.

'To steely determination. And outrageous progress.'

Robbie laughed, taking a sip from her glass.

'That's nice, thank you. Particularly as you don't hold with the steely determination part.'

He shrugged. 'Nothing wrong with determination. It's one of the building blocks of recovery.'

'*Steely* determination, though?' Robbie raised her eyebrows.

'I admire steel, too.'

As long as it had the capacity to bend. Their relationship was all about compromise.

'Well, this last couple of days has been a revelation.'

'Yeah? Enlighten me.'

'The questions that people ask, after we think we're done with them. How they feel about their experience.'

He nodded. 'Maybe you should write it all up. It sounds as if this could turn into something that we could all benefit from.'

He'd been nothing but positive about this. If Dr Thompson had intended Robbie's amended work role as a placebo, then it didn't really matter because Joel had turned it into something that was working, and that had been a learning exercise for both Robbie and the whole department.

'I hope I won't be doing this for long enough to be writing anything up.'

'That's not really up to you, is it?' He leaned

back in his seat, looking thoughtfully out at the bird feeder at the end of the garden, where despite their presence a robin had alighted.

Robbie puffed out a sigh. 'I don't do well with things I can't control.'

His grin broadened suddenly. 'A control freak. Tell me more…'

She wasn't going to tell him about how she might bend his body to her will. Or how he might bend hers. Even if the touch of mischief in his melting eyes brought that right to the forefront of her thoughts.

But could she reveal more about why she kept such tight control over her life and her emotions? Why that made things easier.

'I've had eczema since I was a kid. I didn't think too much of it, apart from when it got really itchy. Getting to be a teenager changed things.'

'You mean that agonising feeling that everyone's looking at you?'

Everyone *had* been looking at her. The newspaper article had seen to that, and it had shown her that anonymity was her best protection.

'What were you self-conscious about when you were a teenager?' Robbie couldn't imagine Joel having too much to worry about.

He chuckled. 'Just the normal stuff. I grew

eight inches in two years and I was clumsier than a baby giraffe.'

He'd made up for that since. Joel was tall, but he'd knitted together well, with a controlled power that made him a pleasure to look at.

'That's not the same, though. People expect teenaged boys to be a bit gawky.' He seemed to understand, without having to be told. It seemed easy to acknowledge the things she never talked about.

'Yes, that's the thing. Something that's slightly different from everyone else gives some people the idea that you belong to them, and they can talk about you however they like.'

'That's such bad manners,' he quipped.

Joel never failed to make her smile, and she liked that he thought about it like that. 'Yes. All about them and not about me.'

He looked at her thoughtfully. 'But it's you that it hurts.'

'It did hurt a lot, when I was a teenager. Now it just makes me…weary. I can deal with my eczema myself and I can't be bothered about engaging with other people's negative attitudes.'

He was nodding thoughtfully. Waiting. That was Joel's modus operandi; she'd seen him when he was at work. He just waited and people told him things. But this was different. He wasn't gathering information, he just wanted to understand and inhabit the same mental space as her.

'Boyfriends. I found that I couldn't deal with their negative attitudes, actually.'

There was a flash of understanding in his eyes. 'Ah. Yes, it's the relationships that always get you, isn't it? Boys are horrible. You can take my word for that. I used to be one.'

'Don't categorise yourself. Not everyone's like that. Sometimes they are…'

'Yeah. Sometimes.' He was still waiting. Robbie drew in a breath.

'I had this guy… I was in my last year at university and there was a bit of pressure, and my eczema was flaring up a lot more than it does now. He used to make a big thing about me dressing to cover it when I went out, and there were even times he made an excuse about not turning up for things when my eczema was really noticeable. He used to tell me that I needed to change my clothes, or apply more make-up if he could see any red patches.'

'And you gave him his marching orders…?' Joel's face hardened suddenly. 'Didn't you?'

It hadn't been that easy. Robbie had been young and she'd craved acceptance from the person that she'd thought she loved. *Had* loved. It was Rory who hadn't loved her well enough.

'It took me a while. I really liked him, but not being good enough for him as I was didn't do much for my confidence.'

'I'd say he wasn't anywhere near good enough for you.' The way his lips caressed the words seemed to scream the message that the tender look in his eyes was giving.

'I think...it wasn't really about the practicalities, although he made it all about that. It was about him, and the way he was. What he wanted out of things.'

Joel considered the thought. 'What *did* he want?'

'A mouse. Someone who did what he said and reckoned they were lucky to have him.'

He laughed suddenly. 'Okay, you definitely failed at that. There are a lot of words I'd use to describe you, but *mouse* never occurred to me.'

It would be interesting to know what words Joel would use to describe her. Maybe she was falling into the same trap all over again, and craving his approval. Or maybe it would just be interesting...

Robbie wondered if she should tell him about the rest of it. Her parents' money, and how that had catapulted her into the public gaze. Rory's attitude to the money, and the suspicions that it was all he'd ever really seen in her.

But secrets had saved her life. They were the comfortable cushion that protected her, and which allowed her to be seen for what she did, and not who she was. Letting go of one of them might not be so bad, but letting go of everything was impossibly risky.

'I decided not to be a mouse any more. The funny thing was that when I applied my own solution to the problem, and left him, my eczema improved a lot. It has a habit of getting worse when I'm stressed out.'

He nodded. 'And now you need to be in control of your recovery, because taking things into your own hands is what's worked for you in the past.'

It seemed that he really did get it. Maybe he'd get the rest of it, as well, but Robbie didn't have it in her to explain. How she'd felt that she was disappearing under the weight of other people's expectations. And how actually disappearing had changed all of that, and allowed her to expect other people to take her as they found her.

'I'm working on it. By the time I'm better, I'll be a model patient.'

He chuckled. 'And in the meantime you'll be a terrible patient.'

'Maybe. Sorry.'

'Don't be. I can only take so many good

patients in a day and then I find I need someone to stretch me a bit. You reckon it's about time to eat?'

Yes. She'd told him enough already, and there was such a thing as quitting while you were ahead.

'I'm really hungry. I'm getting far too used to three square meals a day.'

'Good. How do you feel about home-made hamburgers? I'd do them on the barbecue, as a last-ditch attempt to preserve the summer, but I'm not sure how my neighbours might react to barbequing at nine o'clock on a Saturday morning.'

'Hamburgers sound great. And thanks for the talk.'

'I didn't say all that much.' That innocent look of his always made her insides go to jelly.

'You're going down in my estimation if you think that. Quick, go cook…'

He held up his hands in a gesture of surrender, and disappeared back into the kitchen.

CHAPTER SIX

JOEL COULDN'T SHAKE the feeling that Robbie was holding something back. The way she'd thought so carefully during the silences between them, as if choosing her words. He knew all about those silences and the guilty feeling that his parents' marriage hung on what he chose to say next. He knew that he'd never had the guts to say what was on his mind, even though his mother had sometimes seemed to know. Even though he'd wanted so badly for the words to fall from his mouth. And he knew that he couldn't stand the idea that Robbie was keeping secrets from him.

He pushed the thought aside. He could understand being hurt and his heart ached for the way that Robbie had been hurt. That was all there was to it.

He made hamburgers with bacon and cheese, salad, French fries and onion rings. The look on Robbie's face when he brought the plates out was worth the twenty minutes he'd spent out of the reach of her gaze.

'You are a *dream*! Do you always cut your hamburgers into four?'

'No. I thought you might feel that I was singling you out for special treatment if I didn't cut mine up as well.' Teasing her was becoming one of his favourite pastimes. And Robbie was one of those people who only seemed to take offence at things that weren't said.

'Good thought. My feelings are completely salvaged.' She picked up a quarter of her hamburger and took a bite. 'Mmm. This is so good.'

'Sauce…' Some of the sauce was dribbling down her chin. He leaned forward to hand her a napkin and she stuck her chin out playfully, not letting go of the hamburger.

He rolled his eyes, pretending that wiping her chin for her was a chore. But the look in her eyes was one of sheer nakedness, and it exploded through him.

'I was thinking…'

'Should I be worried?' He grinned at her.

'You tell me. It's been really good of you to bring me to and from work this last couple of days, but I thought that next week I ought to go into work on the Tube. What do you reckon?'

'I think that's a terrible idea. It's a ten-minute detour for me to pick you up. I'd far rather do that than be fretting about whether someone's crashed into you on the Tube and you're howling in agony somewhere. And I've got used to having you around. I quite like the company.'

Sometimes the direct approach was the most effective. It certainly was with Robbie; she looked as if that was the last answer she'd expected from him.

'You're not going to lecture me about taking things easy?'

'You've had those lectures already. And I was listening when you were talking earlier about defining your own needs, rather than responding to someone else's. So I reckoned I'd just tell you *my* needs and let you pitch in with yours.'

Robbie stared at him. And then she laughed. 'You listen far too well, Joel.'

Nice. That was a nice thing to say. He *did* listen to every word that Robbie said. It was difficult not to.

'So what *are* your needs?'

She shot him a look of indescribable mischief. 'I listened to you, too. I need to lighten up and actually get better, instead of pretending there's nothing wrong with me. I'd appreciate a lift to and from work next week, if that's okay with you.'

'It would be my pleasure.'

Something had changed between them and Joel reckoned that it suited them. They were clearing away the old patterns of the past, and it gave them just that bit more space to inhabit together. And right now, time and space with Robbie was all he really wanted.

Joel could hear the little boy howling. The whole of the A & E department could hear him, even though he was with Kat and up till now Joel had reckoned that it was impossible for a child to resist Kat's reassurance, and still continue to cry.

'Bring him back.' The woman he was trying to treat batted his hands away and sat painfully up on the bed. 'He needs to be with me.'

'Sarah, I need to take a look at you.' Joel tried to reason with her.

'No! You don't touch me until I've seen my son.'

Common sense told him that you didn't examine a woman who'd fallen down the stairs, and who might well have any number of injuries, with her five-year-old son in the cubicle. It appeared that common sense wasn't going to work.

'Okay. Stay here, right? I'll go and fetch him.' Joel glanced at the nurse who was helping him, and she nodded. He left the cubicle, hoping that the child's cries had attracted the attention of the one person he wanted to see.

They had. The door of the next cubicle was open, and Robbie was already there. Kat was kneeling down next to Sarah's son, who was crouched in the corner, sobbing his heart out.

First things first. Joel needed to defuse the situation, before he talked to Robbie, whose experience of dealing with children in distress in the paediatric A & E unit might well come in useful at the moment.

'Kat, why don't you take him in to see his mum for a minute? We can't do anything for either of them like this.'

Kat nodded, bending down to speak to the boy. As soon as she said the word *'mother'* he got to his feet, allowing her to lead him out of the cubicle, his face still bright red and tears still running down his cheeks.

'What's the story? Kat's usually so good with kids.' Robbie looked up at him, concern on her face.

'They came in by ambulance. Mum had fallen down the stairs and her son got out of bed and brought her phone to her so she could call for help.'

'Brave kid. How is she?'

'Difficult to say—she's not letting me examine her. She says that Eliot has to be with her. He's been through a lot and he's obviously upset and worried, but we gave him and his mum plenty of time together and I explained that she was all right. I've never seen this level of separation anxiety before in either a parent or a child.'

Robbie thought for a moment. 'Is he neuro-divergent?'

'I asked and his mum says not. There's an issue here that I haven't been able to address and I'd like to be able to calm Eliot's fears, but his mum won't say anything more than he just wants to be with her.'

'They were alone in the house?'

'They were when the ambulance got there. They brought Eliot in because they wanted him checked over by Paediatrics, but every time he loses sight of her he starts screaming and there's no calming him down. I'd really appreciate your input.'

Robbie shot him a smile, and he began to feel a bit more equal to the situation. 'Okay, let's do this. I'll take Eliot through the basic checks you'll be doing on his mum. Maybe he'll feel better if he sees he's a little more in control of the process.'

'Yeah. That works.' It struck a chord with Joel, as well, from somewhere way back in his own experience. Being in control, rather than just responsible for a myriad of bad outcomes, had been something he'd wanted as a kid.

'If it looks as if something's happening that we don't want Eliot to see, then give me some warning if you can.' Robbie nudged him gently back into the here and now.

'Will do.' Joel looked across to the other cubicle. Kat had ushered Eliot inside, and the grizzling had stopped, as if someone had flipped a switch.

An exchanged glance told him that Robbie was concerned too. She followed him into the cubicle and Joel saw that Kat had lifted Eliot up to sit with his mother. Sarah was talking to him quietly and the boy was smiling now, even though his face was still red from his tears.

Robbie walked over to the pair. 'I'm looking for a boy called Eliot. I'm Dr Robbie.'

Eliot eyed her suspiciously. 'You've got a boy's name.'

'Yes, that's right. I'll tell you my real name if you like.'

She whispered in Eliot's ear and he nodded. Joel dismissed the temptation to ask Robbie to share the secret with all of them. It was just a way of helping Eliot feel a little more in control of things, and it seemed to be working.

'Did you hurt your hand?'

Eliot reached out to touch Robbie's arm gently, and she didn't flinch back, as she usually did when it looked as if someone was coming too close. She was wearing a light sling that gave her more freedom of movement but still supported her shoulder, and she lifted her forearm a little, wiggling her fingers.

'No, but I hurt my shoulder, so I have to wear this for a while.' She wrinkled her nose in an expression that Joel always found irresistible. 'I fell off my bike. Dr Joel fixed my shoulder for me though, and it felt much better straight away.'

Eliot nodded. 'My mum fell. From the top of the stairs to the bottom.'

'I heard that you were a very brave boy, and that you went to fetch her phone so that your mum could call for an ambulance.' Robbie leaned in confidingly, her voice dropping to little more than a whisper. 'Dr Joel's going to look after your mum too. He's the best doctor in the hospital but don't tell him I said that.'

'Why not?'

'He'll get a big head. But since he *is* the best doctor in the hospital, then I think it would be okay if he looks after your mum, don't you?'

Eliot looked Joel up and down gravely, and he smiled at the boy encouragingly.

'What's he going to do?' Eliot didn't seem convinced.

'Let's see now...' Robbie pretended to think for a moment. 'Why don't we ask Dr Joel to tell us exactly what he needs to check out with your mum? We'll try it out as well, so that you know whether it's okay.'

The same thing that had occurred to Joel was behind Robbie's suggestion. Eliot had seen someone hurt his mum, and the boy was trying to protect her. To him, Joel wasn't a doctor, but an unknown threat to his mother.

Eliot nodded, and Robbie glanced across at Sarah. 'Is that all right?'

'Yes. Thank you.' Sarah took her son's hand. 'You go with the lady doctor, Eliot. I'll be right here.'

This was the signal to move. Robbie stood back and Kat picked Eliot up, giving him a cuddle before she set him down on a chair on the other side of the cubicle. And Joel took his place next to Sarah.

'I'm sorry...he just needed to see me.'

'That's all right. He's had a fright, and so have you.' Joel smiled reassuringly, raising his voice so that both Eliot and Robbie could hear him. 'Now I'd like to just check your ribs...'

* * *

Sarah's gaze didn't leave her son, and Joel had to catch her attention a couple of times before she answered his questions. But they were making progress. Robbie was carefully following his lead and with Kat's help she was managing to examine Eliot thoroughly in the process. The boy was obviously encouraged by feeling involved with what was happening to his mum, and called across to her from time to time, to tell her that everything was okay. From Robbie's quiet words, it appeared that he had no physical injuries.

Sarah, on the other hand, hadn't been so lucky. Her ankle was swelling badly, and was almost certainly fractured, and so was one wrist. She had badly bruised ribs and a slight concussion and Joel was going to have to keep her in the hospital overnight at least. He relayed the news to her and asked if there was anyone who could take care of Eliot.

'I'll call my mum. She'll take him.' Sarah glanced across at Eliot, who was whispering something to Robbie. 'Oh, dear...'

'What is it, Sarah?' Robbie had been giving Eliot her full attention, but there was something about the way that she was leaning towards the boy, listening carefully to what he was saying, that was ringing alarm bells.

'I don't know what to do...' Sarah looked up at him, biting her lip in agitation.

'Is there a problem with having your mum look after Eliot?'

'No...no, Mum's really good with him and he adores my dad. They only live five minutes away from me, and they look after Eliot all the time.'

'He won't mind leaving you here?'

'No, you've been so good with him and...he had a shock but he's feeling much more confident now. He'll be all right if he's with Mum and Dad. I just...' Sarah's hand moved to her mouth to cover her sobs.

Silences, and the pain that inhabited them. The things that weren't said, which ate into you if you weren't careful.

'Are you and Eliot covering up for anyone, Sarah?'

Sarah nodded, her gaze moving behind him to her son. Joel looked round and saw Robbie curling her arm around the boy's shoulders, and when she glanced up at him their gazes met. In that moment, Joel knew that he was going to have to give a little of himself, to protect the child.

'Sarah, I think that Eliot has to talk about this. There's one thing that you can do to make it easier for him.'

'You think…?'

'I know it's hard for you, but please don't let him carry this on his own.'

'It was my ex… Eliot's father.' Sarah whispered the words. 'He pushed me and Eliot saw. I told him not to say anything. I didn't want him to have to speak up against his father…'

The nurse on the other side of the bed was comforting Sarah as best she could. Joel didn't want to ask, but he had to.

'Has he hurt either you or Eliot before?'

'No. Never.'

It was always best to be honest and clear about what he needed to do next. 'Okay. As Eliot saw his father push you, the law requires that I report that because I have to put his interests above anything else. It's up to you whether you press charges or want to get the police involved, but that might be something to consider.'

Sarah nodded. 'I suppose if you *have* to report it… Just as long as you do what you said. Put Eliot's interests first.'

'That's what everyone here will do. We have a dedicated team here at the hospital and there's a domestic violence advisor on call right now. She's very experienced in dealing with this kind of situation and I'd like to ask her to come down and speak with you, if that's okay.'

'I don't know...' A tear ran down Sarah's cheek. 'It all seems so... I don't think it's really necessary to talk to domestic violence people. He's never done this before.'

'No, but he's done it now. He hasn't just hurt you, he's hurt Eliot and we want to make sure that he can mend, too. No one's going to draw conclusions or try to classify you, but I do think you need some help right now.'

Sarah nodded. 'Yes, you're right. I want to see her, then. On the condition that Eliot's her first concern, because I'm his mother and he's *my* first concern.'

Something about the vehemence of Sarah's whispered words made Joel smile. 'All right. I'll go and call her now, and then we'll get you down to X-ray.'

He left Sarah with the nurse and waited for a moment outside the cubicle. As he'd expected, Robbie came outside to join him.

'What did Eliot have to say for himself?'

She turned the corners of her mouth down. 'That his father pushed his mother down the stairs. He hasn't hurt Eliot before, and from what I can see that's the case. He's an extremely healthy little boy and he doesn't have a mark on him. Which is pretty unusual, actually, for a five-year-old. Sarah?'

'She said the same. And that Eliot saw what happened.'

Robbie let out an exclamation of dismay. 'That poor kid.'

'And that she'd told Eliot to keep quiet about it, because she didn't want him to have to say anything against his father.' Joel could understand why Sarah had done it, but he knew from his own experience just how agonising it was to be a child with a secret.

'Okay. I can see why she did that, she was trying to protect him, but he did need to talk about it. All I had to do was gain his confidence a little and he just told me. I didn't have to push him.'

'Sarah saw him whispering to you, and she realised that she couldn't keep it a secret.' Joel wondered what it would have been like if someone like Robbie had taken the time to gain *his* confidence as a child. His own story was still waiting to be heard, and he could hardly bear it at the moment.

'You're calling the domestic violence advisor?'

'Yeah. I guess she'll take it from here.' There was nothing more to be said. There were strict procedures, designed to protect both Eliot and Sarah, that everyone would follow from here on. Somehow Joel just couldn't let go of it, though.

'What?' Robbie seemed to know that he wasn't done with this.

'I just… You know how it is. Some cases just get to you.' He shrugged. 'You must deal with these kinds of cases, where kids are involved, all the time.'

'Not all of the time, but we have our share of them. If I ever get used to it, then I'll know I'm in a lot of trouble.' She took a step closer to him. 'There's a procedure for this. Meet me outside the staff entrance, when it's time for our break.'

'Break? What's a break? We're pretty busy tonight.'

Robbie smiled. 'You'll find the time. Call me when you do.'

Phillipa, the duty domestic violence advisor, was with another family and so Robbie had volunteered to stay with Sarah and Eliot until she was free. Eliot had been snuggling sleepily against his mother for most of the time, but Robbie had managed to coax him away from her for long enough for the X-rays to be taken.

When the results came through, Joel returned to the cubicle and quietly explained to Sarah that the X-rays had shown her ankle and wrist were fractured, telling her exactly what would happen next. His reassuring manner had made Sarah and Eliot feel safe and secure, and when Phillipa finally arrived, Sarah was ready to take the action that was needed to protect herself and her son.

'Two minutes…' Robbie murmured the words as she walked past him, as he strode towards the administration desk to file his notes.

'Three…' He called after her and Robbie decided it would probably be four.

It was five, but just as she was beginning to shiver in the cool night air, he made it. He was smiling but there was an edge of weariness about Joel, as if he'd been fighting with his thoughts.

'Here's what we're going to do. First you take a deep breath.' She sucked in a lungful of air, and puffed it back out again and Joel followed suit.

'Second, you say the first thing that comes into your mind.'

'Are you making this up as you go along?' He raised an eyebrow.

'Yes, I am. Just do it…'

'Your eyes are a deeper blue in this light.'

Were they? 'Is that *really* the first thing that came to mind?'

'Yes. What's yours?'

'I just told you…' Robbie decided that pursuing that would only tie them up in knots and that she should move on.

'Then it's the group hug.'

Joel made a point of looking around for any groups that might have suddenly appeared. There was no one else here. Then he smiled, folding his arms gently around her, careful not to jostle her injured shoulder.

It wasn't *quite* a group hug. For a start there were too few people, but that wouldn't have mattered so much. Snuggling against him, hearing his heart beat… Not wanting to let him go, and being able to believe that he couldn't let her go either. Feeling a heady intoxication, instead of just comfort.

'This works.' He was looking down at her, and Robbie thought she saw the reflection of a kiss in his eyes.

For one heady moment, all she could think about was that they might run away. That they'd race to his car, and he'd drive to her apartment and if the lift travelled fast enough they'd just about make it to the front door before they were making sweet love.

It was a nice thought, and it was just as well that it hadn't occurred to her earlier because then she would have had to confess that it was the first thought that came to mind. And there were people waiting for them. Not just tonight, but every night. This was what they'd built their lives around; it was what they were. Robbie let go of him, and felt Joel's arms loosen.

'Are we ready to go back…?' She couldn't avoid his gaze.

'You go inside, you're shivering. I can do with a few more breaths.'

'You're all right, though?'

'I'm fine. This really works, thank you. I just want a little time alone.'

These few moments of respite hadn't been enough. They'd been so delicious that they felt like for ever, but Robbie had the feeling that whatever was nagging at Joel had just been submerged, and not completely banished.

It happened. Bad things happened and some of them would push buttons for the medical professionals who were doing their best to help people. You picked yourself back up again and kept going, because if you didn't then more bad things would happen to more people.

Something about Sarah and Eliot had pushed buttons with Joel, but when she saw him return to the admin desk to pick up the notes for his next patient, he seemed to have pulled himself back together. He caught her staring at him and smiled, mouthing a *thank you* across the busy space. That was all she really needed to know.

CHAPTER SEVEN

NIGHTSHIFTERS HADN'T BEEN busy tonight, and there were plenty of people to deal with the calls that were coming in. Joel had taken Robbie home, on the understanding that the two of them would be on standby, in case they were needed.

Which was why Robbie was cooking at half past one in the morning. That seemed to involve a great deal of mess, a long list of printed instructions, and some crashing and cursing floating out from the kitchen. In the end, Joel decided that staying in the sitting room was far too much to ask of him.

'What the…?' When he walked into the kitchen, the mess seemed to have grown exponentially since Robbie had chased him away. Since she could still only lift anything with her left arm, she'd clearly skipped past the expediency of putting anything away again when she'd found what she wanted, and it looked as if half the contents of her kitchen cupboards were strewn across the worktops.

'I know. This is my sister's recipe, and she says it's really quick and easy. Izzy never mentioned the mess.' She shifted her arm in the sling to hold up her hands in an expression of surrender. Which wasn't really surrender at all; she was holding her hands up because she could. Robbie never missed a chance to demonstrate how her shoulder had been improving over the last week.

'I expect when you've done it a few times, you'll know exactly what you need…' He started to put some of the unused kitchen implements back into the cupboard. 'You have a sister?'

He couldn't help asking. Robbie had given the same smile when she mentioned her sister as she had when she talked about her parents and it seemed that her family were close. Joel was happy for her, and at the same time a little envious.

'Yes, we don't get to see each other all that much because Izzy and her husband live in Ireland. But we talk all the time and she's a great cook. I've been thinking for a while that I might give it a go as a hobby, and since I have some extra time…'

Joel nodded. It was just as well that this was

a hobby, because none of the effort that Robbie was putting into it was in the least practical.

'What are you making?' Joel couldn't decide from the array of ingredients and utensils that were scattered around the kitchen.

'Chocolate cake.' Robbie flipped through several sheets of paper, which contained typed instructions and photographs of every stage of the process, and stabbed her finger against the final one. 'I don't think it's going to look like this.'

'I don't see why not. Just follow the instructions and it'll be great. Want me to stack the dishwasher?'

'That sounds like helping to me, Joel. The idea of baking is that I get some time alone in the kitchen to express my creativity. Creativity always involves mess. You can't do it without breaking a few eggs…' She grinned at him. 'See what I did, there?'

He couldn't help smiling. 'Yeah, I saw. Can't hurt to share a piece of your creativity, can it?' Whatever Robbie did, she did with an intoxicating verve. It was impossible to just walk away and cool his heels in the sitting room.

'That was going to be when I presented you with a slice, so you could have the first taste.'

'If I'm going to get the first taste, it's only

fair to let me see what you're putting into it, isn't it?' he teased, and Robbie wrinkled her nose.

'It's all there, in the mixer bowl.' Robbie gestured towards a mixer that looked as if it might also make you a cup of tea and sing a lullaby if you selected the correct programme. 'Izzy said it was okay to do it like this, since it's bit tricky to do the mixing myself with only one good arm.'

She consulted a bulky instruction booklet and turned a knob on the top of the mixer. The paddles started to move, and, after squinting into the bowl, Robbie clearly decided it was best to let the machine get on with it.

'What's this?' Joel caught sight of a bowl that contained a dark, chocolatey substance, and wondered if Robbie had forgotten to add it to the rest of the ingredients.

'Oh, that's the topping. I decided to do it first, because it looked the easiest.'

Okay. Whatever worked. Robbie walked over to him, dipping her finger into the bowl and licking it. That worked too...

'I'm not sure if it's a bit too runny.' She rubbed the side of her nose, leaving a chocolate smear. He could resist that. Then she pushed a stray curl out of her eyes, leaving a trace of the mixture on her forehead. *That* wasn't playing fair.

'You've got it all over you, now. No…don't touch, let me…' He picked up a kitchen towel, wiping the gooey mixture from her face, but when some of it got onto his fingers he couldn't resist taking a taste.

'It's good… The icing's good.'

Then he was lost in her gaze, pale sapphire tonight under the bright kitchen lights. Robbie's mouth curled into a mischievous grin.

'That's not enough to tell, is it?' She dipped her finger in the bowl again, holding her hand up towards him.

A rich, chocolatey taste on his tongue, and the feel of her body against his as she stepped closer. Then Joel did what he'd been aching to do since the first moment he'd seen Robbie, and kissed her.

If he'd had time to consider what he was doing he might have prepared himself for an anticlimax, because it would be logical to suppose that nothing could be quite as good as what had been going on in his imagination. Logical thought could go take a running jump, because this was better. Sweeter. More unexpected and unrehearsed.

She moved against him, curling one hand behind his neck, the other arm tucked against his chest in the sling. Robbie stretched up, standing on her toes, and he felt the delicious slide of friction between them. That intoxicating feeling that he was losing his balance and falling into a place where there was only the two of them, and Robbie was kissing him.

'You taste of chocolate.' She must like that, because she kissed him again. She tasted of...

A different life. One that saw no limit on how he might give himself to her. One that didn't recognise the fear that had bound him and kept him in solitary confinement for years. If she hadn't hesitated before the next kiss, just for one moment, he would have been free.

But she did. And her hesitation allowed the doubts in. Robbie had been hurt and even though she seemed bold in so many areas of her life, she was also cautious. The next step, the one that seemed almost inevitable now, was the one that could hurt her even more if fear made him stick to what he knew and draw back again.

'You are so perfect...' He caressed her cheek tenderly, staring into her eyes. 'And I am...so fearful.'

Her eyes darkened suddenly, with an emotion that he couldn't quite get the measure of.

'Why?'

'I know you've been hurt. I've been hurt too and I can't do this without telling you…'

'Then tell me, Joel.'

He didn't know how to answer. Joel knew how corrosive secrets could be, but it was hard to let go of this one. He knew that he had to, before he embarked on any kind of physical relationship with Robbie.

His phone rang in his back pocket, and he ignored it. He didn't care what Glen, or anyone else, wanted. The whole world could crash and burn, as long as they could have just a few more moments together.

She grimaced and reached round, pulling the phone from his pocket. As she did so, it stopped ringing.

'Missed it…'

He spoke too soon, and his phone started to ring again. Robbie flipped the answer button and handed the phone to him.

'Hello…?' His voice sounded husky and strange.

'Joel? Sorry, were you in the middle of something? It's Glen.'

'No, it's okay.' Joel pulled himself together, the effort greater than it might have been, because his other hand was still around Robbie's waist. 'What can we do?'

'Is Rob with you?'

'Yes, she's here.'

'We need to get an organ donation, from Tower Bridge to Birmingham. Are you up for it? You'll need to have Rob with you, because she's a named person on our agreement to carry organs.'

'Okay, I'll check and call you back.' He glanced at Robbie. 'Transplant organ from London to Birmingham?'

'Yes! Of course…' Robbie stepped back suddenly. Losing her was almost a physical shock, as if something had been ripped away from him. Then he heard Glen's voice at the other end of the line.

'I heard. Call me back when you're ready to go.'

Joel put his phone back into his pocket. 'I didn't know Nightshifters did organ transport.'

'Yeah, we don't do a lot of them, but their usual carriers must be busy. We have an agreement in place, and because we're volunteers we had to submit a list of named people.'

'And this is okay with you…?'

'What do you think?' She grinned at him as if someone had just presented her with a surprise gift. 'Let's go to Birmingham.'

Robbie switched off the mixer, and put the bowl into the sink, reckoning that there would be no salvaging the cake when they got back. Joel had already fetched their coats, and on the way downstairs in the lift he was on the phone with Glen, getting the details of where they were to go and who they should ask for when they got there. They were in the car within two minutes.

Two minutes when everything had suddenly changed again, back to what they'd been before. There was no thinking about that, and they had to postpone whatever it was that Joel wanted to talk about. He understood that the urgency of their work sometimes took priority, just as well as she did, and he knew that there would be time to talk later.

'We'll avoid Covent Garden, cut across to the City and then Waterloo.'

'Okay.' He shot her a grin. 'Directions?'

Joel knew his way around London, but Robbie had a better grasp of which shortcuts to take and how to avoid the traffic. Covent Garden would still be busy at this time on a Saturday night, but the City of London would be deserted.

Tall, glass-clad buildings, and older granite monoliths loomed up on either side of them. Joel was driving at just under the speed limit, and they'd be in good time to collect the kidney that was being removed and prepared for transport in the hospital on the other side of the river.

'This is one of the things I like about working at night. You get to see the same things in a completely different way.' He nodded towards the clear road ahead of him.

'Me too.'

This part of London was usually full of people and traffic during the day. At night, the quiet solidity of the buildings was all that remained of that frenetic activity. They were alone here in their small bubble, and it seemed that all of London was theirs, from tin tabernacles to royal palaces.

Robbie looked to her left as they crossed Waterloo Bridge, to see Tower Bridge, swathed with lights, further up the river. She saw Joel glance that way too, and smile. It was as if it were glimmering in the darkness just for them.

There were IDs to be checked, and paperwork to be completed at the hospital, then a half-hour wait until the kidney was ready to be transported. Then their precious cargo, labelled and sealed, was handed to Joel and they hurried to the car. He secured the organ transport box inside the Nightshifters carrier on the back seat, while Robbie called the Tin Tabernacle to confirm that they were on their way to Birmingham.

They left the lights of London behind, and Robbie settled back into her seat, no longer needing to give directions now that they were on the motorway. Joel had opened one of the windows by a crack, for some fresh air to keep him alert, and she wrapped her jacket around her for warmth.

'Twenty-four to thirty-six hours…' The numbers had been running through her head, since they first took charge of the kidney, and she was hardly aware that she'd voiced the time that a kidney would remain viable for transplant.

Joel chuckled. 'We're not going to need that long. We'll be there in a few hours, tops.'

'We're not there, until we're there.' This was the first time she'd been on a delivery since her accident. The long walk from the side gate of the hospital to where Joel had found her outside A & E suddenly seemed very clear in her mind.

'Hey. We'll be there.'

She had the comforting thrum of the SUV's engine, which was effortlessly eating up the miles. An empty motorway in front of them. And most of all she wasn't alone this time, because she had Joel.

He leaned forward, flipping on the radio. The late-night talk show was about as soporific as the motorway floodlights that flashed past at regular intervals.

'Can you find some music?' He glanced in her direction, and Robbie smiled back at him.

'Driving music?'

He chuckled. 'Of course, driving music. What else?'

They arrived in Birmingham just over two hours later, and Joel was still humming the last track that had been playing in the car as they hurried to the transplant unit at the hospital. They'd called ahead to say when they'd be arriving, and a junior surgeon was waiting for them at Reception.

The box was checked for any damage, times and dates were recorded and Robbie scribbled her signature at the bottom of a form. The young man hurried away, the next link in a chain that would bring hope to someone.

'Is there somewhere we can get a drink and something to eat?' Robbie asked the nurse who'd been there to witness the handover document.

'You could try the cafeteria, but at this time of night it's all leftover sandwiches. Turn right out of the main gates and go three hundred yards and there's a little takeaway café. It doesn't look much from the outside, but it's much better.'

'Great, thanks. Have a good night.'

'Wait…' They'd already turned to leave but the nurse called them back. 'I heard that you're both volunteers?'

'Yes, we work with a charity called Night-shifters in North London.'

'Thank you, on behalf of a great kid and their family.'

Joel grinned broadly. This meant as much to him as it did to Robbie. The nurse couldn't say any more, but she'd given them all the information they needed.

'It's our pleasure. Thank *you*.'

They parked outside a rather ramshackle-looking café, and Robbie wondered whether Joel would be straight back out again after he'd seen the inside of the place. But when he returned to the car he was carrying coffee and a brown paper bag.

'That place is amazing inside. It's got the old-style green and white tiles on the walls, with scrubbed wooden tables and stools—it's like stepping back in time. It's spotless though, and they have a great selection of food.'

Robbie laughed. 'Another little hidden gem of the night.'

'Yep.' He handed her his purchases and started the car.

He seemed to know where he was going and he drew up, five minutes later, by the side of a large warehouse building that had been re-purposed into smart flats. On the other side of the road there was a railing, and beyond that the glint of water.

'A river?'

Joel rolled his eyes. 'No. Birmingham doesn't have any navigable rivers. It has loads of canals, though.'

'And you knew how to get here by instinct?' Robbie followed him out of the car, and onto a small footbridge.

'No, I worked in Birmingham for a couple of years. How does standing and eating sound?'

'Like heaven.' They'd been in the car for long enough now, and Robbie wanted to stretch her legs.

He stopped in the middle of the bridge and propped the coffees on the curved iron parapet, then opened the bag. Just the smell made her mouth water. She opened the greaseproof-paper package that Joel had given her and took a bite from the toasted cheese and tomato sandwich.

'Mmm. That's really good. So what were you doing in Birmingham?' Joel hardly ever spoke about anything other than the present and the future, and she'd never heard him mention his family.

'Just working. There was a good job here, and I took it.'

'And London?'

He shrugged. 'Same, really. There was another good job and I took it. I like London and so I stayed. Then the job at the London Fitzrovia hospital came up, and I couldn't pass it up. There are so many good initiatives going on there.'

He didn't seem to mind her questions. Robbie ventured another.

'Where do you come from?'

'Surrey. I went to medical school in London and there weren't any good jobs in Surrey when I left, so I didn't go back.'

She should stop. She hadn't told him everything about herself, and if Joel wanted to keep something back it was his right to do so. Robbie fell silent, watching the reflection of the streetlights in the dark water below her.

She finished her toastie, rolling the grease-proof paper up into a ball and putting it into her pocket. Joel reached for her coffee, handing it to her.

There was one thing she needed to know, though. He'd kissed her and she'd kissed him back, but she wasn't so naïve as to believe that they would have been waking up together if Glen hadn't called. Joel had already been drawing back from her when his phone had rung.

'What's going on between us, Joel?'

'I kissed you and I meant it.' He seemed to be savouring that moment in his mind as he stared out over the water. 'We've both got our reasons for being cautious.'

'It probably wasn't a good idea.' It had felt like a pretty darn fantastic idea to Robbie, but she sensed that Joel needed a bit of space.

'Maybe not.' He turned the corners of his mouth down. 'Sometimes the bad ideas are the ones you like the most.'

Always the gentleman. Not so much gentleman as gentle man, Joel wouldn't let her feel embarrassed about kissing him.

Maybe it was the eczema...

That came from another place, one where she'd allowed Rory to see only the money and the eczema and not look past either of them. Joel wasn't like that, he never thought about how her eczema affected him he would have found the idea laughable. He only cared about how it affected her.

'Could we make a course correction?' He seemed suddenly embarrassed.

'You mean... Pretend it never happened?'

Joel shook his head, smiling. 'No, let's not do that. Just think of it as something we did on the way to becoming friends?'

He was right. It was what Robbie wanted in her head, it was just her emotions that were running away from her and wanting to beg him to reconsider. That would be a mistake, because she still couldn't shake the way she'd felt when she'd been with Rory.

'Friends is good.' She took his arm as they walked back to the car. But as soon as he unlocked it, opening the passenger door for her, Robbie knew. Things weren't going to be the same between them from now on.

CHAPTER EIGHT

It HAD BEEN a good night's work. It had been great for Robbie too, a chance to get back to doing something that she valued. Joel regretted the kiss, though.

Regret was the wrong word. It had been wonderful, and finding that it was a great deal more wonderful than he'd ever imagined just opened the floodgates on a whole raft of possibilities. What it might be like to wake up with Robbie. To go to sleep with her. All the things they might do together in between waking up and going to sleep.

But he couldn't. The secret that had stood for so many years between him and his family still seemed to surround him. He'd kept lovers at arm's length, and refused to dream about a family of his own because of it. If he couldn't bring himself to see the reproach in Robbie's eyes when he told her, then the secret would just corrode their relationship, the way it had corroded all the others in his life.

They played the same music on the way back to London in the car, but neither of them sang along. Joel dropped Robbie off at her apartment just after dawn and she smiled the way she always did. But he stayed in the car, and she didn't ask him up.

They did all the same things. Joel brought Robbie to work and then took her home again. They exchanged notes on patients, and in the brief moments when there was time for a break they even found themselves drinking coffee and grabbing a sandwich together. But something was missing. They were both being far too friendly, far too polite, and the light in Robbie's eyes had died.

Then Tom and Babs happened. Right at the start of their shift, Joel saw Robbie ushering a middle-aged couple into a cubicle and there was something about the way they were walking close and Robbie was walking right behind them as if to shield them from view that caught his eye. Then he saw a couple of nurses, laughing behind their hands. And then Robbie approached him.

'Got a minute?'

'Yeah, I'm just waiting for some X-rays to come back. What is it?'

'I need a bit of help. I have to lift a patient and I can't do it. But you mustn't laugh.'

'Okay...' Laughing at patients wasn't the norm, although every A & E department had its share of stories about unlikely injuries.

'So... I'm just going to say it. Tom's hand is glued to Babs's bottom. I need to help Babs into a comfortable position where I can get at them to dissolve the glue.'

'Right. This is what we spent seven years studying for, isn't it?'

'Yes, it is.' The corner of Robbie's mouth twitched. 'They're so sweet. If anyone should be glued together it's Tom and Babs, but I'm really worried about the possibility of burns. I looked at the clothing label on Babs' skirt and it doesn't contain cotton, but I still think it's best to get them apart as soon as possible.'

Robbie had a point. A cyanoacrylate adhesive could cause cotton to smoulder or ignite, and he'd seen some nasty injuries where people had dripped glue onto clothing.

'Do we know what kind of glue?'

'No, Tom said it was his model-making glue. His hand's stuck fast, though. The good thing is that neither of them are experiencing any discomfort.'

He followed her to the cubicle. Babs was

perched on the side of the couch, trying not to put too much of her weight on Tom's hand.

'Hi, I'm Dr Joel Mason.'

Both Tom and Babs smiled at him. 'Tom Freestone. And this is Babs, my wife.'

'I think Dr Mason better take a quick look, if that's okay, Babs. Just so he can see how best to get you comfortable.'

'Yes, of course.' Babs beamed at Robbie, sliding off the couch. 'I bet you're wondering how we managed to do this.'

'We see a lot of unexpected things in A & E.' He glanced at Robbie, who was clearly trying not to laugh.

'Yes, he's wondering.'

Babs chuckled and started to explain, while Joel looked at Tom's fingers. 'Tom loves his model aircraft, and I made him a cup of tea and sat down to see what he was doing...'

'And she sat on the glue.' Tom interjected.

'Yes, there was this pop as the tube burst. I realised what I'd done and jumped up, then Tom managed to get the tube off my skirt.' Babs flicked her hand to indicate an urgency of motion. 'But he didn't realise how much glue there was on my skirt. It had soaked through my skirt to my skin and when he put his hand there...well, here we are.'

Tom nodded. 'I suppose if we were going to

glue ourselves together, we may as well have a story to embarrass the kids with when they come over to lunch on Sunday.'

'Yes. Good point,' Babs agreed.

Joel was beginning to see what Robbie meant. Tom and Babs were dealing with what might well have been an embarrassing situation in the best way possible.

'Right, then. As Dr Hall's said, you're stuck pretty fast, and Tom's hand is at a slightly awkward angle to do this standing up. I think that if we can get you onto the couch and you'll be comfortable lying on your tummy, Babs...?'

'Oh, yes, that's perfectly fine.'

'And then we'll find Tom a chair...'

Tom nodded. 'Thanks. Sitting around with your hand on your wife's bottom seems far better manners than standing, eh, Babs?'

Babs snorted with laughter. 'Always the charmer, Tom.'

Robbie giggled. That was the last straw for Joel's composure and he grinned. He saw the light in Robbie's eyes rekindle and warmth flooded through him.

Robbie adjusted the couch to the right height, and Joel practically had to lift Babs onto it to avoid ripping the glued skin. Then he fetched an adjustable stool, for Tom. A nurse brought a bowl of warm soapy water and a bottle of solvent and Robbie settled down on the other side of the couch, ready to start carefully prying Tom and Babs apart.

'I have to go.'

'Yes, thanks, Joel.' Robbie gave him one of her dizzying smiles.

'Thank you...' Tom and Babs chorused as he left the cubicle.

He couldn't help going back. By the time he'd finished dealing with his patient Robbie had managed to prise Tom's fingers free and just the palm of his hand remained stuck. The indomitable pair were still smiling, and Tom's fingers were a little red but there was no real damage to the skin. Robbie flashed him a grin.

Joel went back again, after he'd dealt with his next patient, and found Tom and Babs finally separated. Babs had clearly had the foresight to bring a pair of trousers along with her to wear on the way home and had changed into them.

'Hello again.' Babs gave him a bright smile. 'I'm glad you came back. Robbie says we can go and I wanted to say goodbye and thank you.'

'You're very welcome. None the worse for wear, eh?'

Babs leaned towards him. 'I've got a handprint on my derriere.'

Robbie chuckled. 'The skin's just a bit irritated from the glue. It should fade in the next day or so.'

'More's the pity,' Babs said in mock dismay. 'Thank you so much, Robbie. And for the advice on moisturisers, that was all very handy to know.'

'My pleasure. I hope I don't see you back here any time soon.'

'I'm going to keep well away from him in future.' Babs smiled up at Tom and he put his arm around her shoulders as they left the cubicle.

The door closed, and Joel turned to see Robbie shaking with laughter. 'Oh… I'm so glad they're all right.'

Joel chuckled. 'Me too. How on earth did you manage to keep your hand steady?'

'I have *no* idea. They were both cracking jokes the whole time. And when Babs saw the handprint…she was so pleased with it.' Robbie was laughing and fanning her face at the same time.

Her hand moved to her shoulder and her laughter subsided. Joel suddenly couldn't bear being this far away from Robbie, and moving closer to her wasn't as hard as it had seemed during the last few days. 'You all right? That was a pretty long consult.'

'Yes, I'm okay. I shouldn't laugh so much.' She smiled up at him.

In that moment, Joel knew that he'd been wrong. Acceptance wasn't about the nature of the difficulty, it was about the person you shared it with. He would bide his time, but he *would* tell Robbie his secret, because he trusted that she wouldn't judge and condemn him out of hand. And maybe he'd finally feel free of its burden.

'Yeah. No heavy laughing.' Even if hearing her laugh was the most wonderful thing in the world, right now.

'It's just that… I thought for a moment there that Babs was actually going to show you the handprint, she was so proud of it.' She started to giggle again, and this time Joel couldn't help but laugh with her.

It had been an up and down kind of week. It had started off badly, with awkwardness solidifying into stultifying politeness that felt as if it were freezing Robbie's heart. And then Tom and Babs had turned up. Laughter couldn't cure every ill, but their affectionate jokes and their determination to squeeze humour into their situation had been the catalyst that healed the rift between her and Joel.

The following night Robbie had had to go home early, after a recalcitrant ten-year-old had yanked at her arm when she was trying to examine him. He'd been suffering from a feverish cold, and had probably come out of their encounter in better shape than Robbie had, even if he was a little sleepy and a lot grumpy at being taken from his bed and brought here by his parents.

There was no I-told-you-so from Joel, just the acceptance that accidents happened, and his quiet assurance that the pain would subside. Robbie knew that he was watching her when she returned to work the next night, but she couldn't find it in herself to be indignant. It was just good to have him there and to know that he cared enough to do it.

When he dropped her home after their Friday night shift, she asked him to come inside with her. She had a bottle of prosecco in the fridge, ready to be opened, and she ushered him into the book-lined snug, which was much cosier than the larger, more formal sitting room. They sat on the long sofa together.

'What's this for again?' He twisted the cork out of the bottle, grinning at her.

As if he didn't know. 'Three weeks. I've

done my exercises every day, and, apart from that slight setback the other day, my shoulder feels so much better than it did. And I'm not taking the painkillers any more so I can celebrate with a drink.'

She tipped her glass against his, and they drank together. As lovers did, each not taking their gaze from the other.

He nodded. 'That's a fine piece of progress. It's downhill all the way, now.'

'Downhill? Don't say that, it's supposed to be uphill.'

'Nah. Downhill's a lot easier than uphill. You just take the brakes off and coast.'

'I'm going uphill. Reaching greater heights.'

Joel smiled. 'Whatever floats your boat. Have you read all of these books?' He nodded towards the bookcases that lined the walls.

'No. That's terrible, isn't it…? Having a load of books just sitting here that I haven't read yet.'

'Why? Are you working your way through them?'

'Yes, slowly. Those on the right are mine, and on the other side, the ones with the nicer bindings are my grandparents'. They both read a lot and they had all of the classics.'

'They're a wonderful thing to keep, then, aren't they? You can spend years enjoying the very same books that your grandparents have read. When you've finished, you could go right back to the beginning and read your favourites again.'

'I do think of them sometimes, sitting in here and reading the same things that I am.' Robbie stared at the bubbles that were floating gently upwards in her glass. 'I know how lucky I am.'

He flashed her a quizzical look. 'You make it sound like a bad thing.'

'I don't mean it like that. Just that I'm grateful, because I know that a lot of people aren't given the start in life that I've had.'

'You're one of the hardest-working people I know and you spend your time helping people. If you think you have anything to apologise for, then I'd take issue with that.'

His attitude was like a breath of fresh air. Joel was one of those people who valued someone for what they did, not what they had. It was what Robbie's parents had brought her up to believe.

'I'd find life pretty boring if I didn't do something.'

'Try not to get any more interesting. I'm not sure I can take it, and there aren't enough hours in the day.'

He smiled, raising his hand to brush her

cheek with the backs of his fingers. Robbie shivered. They'd come full circle and were back again in the moment before she'd kissed him, and he'd kissed her back. It was exactly where she wanted to be, but she dreaded the thought that this might be one more iteration in a spiral of intimacy and then disappointment.

She caught his hand in hers. Wanting to keep what she had right now, but not at the cost of losing Joel again. When she looked into his eyes, she knew that they were moments away from repeating a kiss that might be the best thing that could happen, or the worst mistake.

'I don't need to know what's going to happen next, Joel. But I do need to know whether we'll see it through together. I'm sorry if that sounds a bit control freaky...'

He laid his finger across her lips. 'It's nothing of the kind, and I'm just grateful that you're willing to give me a second chance. I won't throw this one away.'

'I know you're cautious and... I like that. I'm cautious too.'

'You should be. You've been hurt before.'

'So have you.' Robbie wanted Joel to know that it was all right to talk and that she'd listen.

'It's...complicated.' He smiled suddenly. 'I think that *complicated* means you have a right to know before we go any further.'

'No, that's not what it means at all. It means you have a right to talk about it if you want. Whenever you want.'

'Then it's my decision to talk about it now.' He reached forward, taking her hand in his. 'Robbie, I don't know where this is all going to lead.'

'Of course you don't. Neither do I. I can't see into the future. But I would very much like to find out.'

CHAPTER NINE

HER EYES WERE sapphire-blue in the firelight. This moment had been inevitable, since the first time they'd met. Waiting to happen, pushed closer by everything they'd said and done.

'When I was seven, I found out that my father was having an affair.'

Shock registered in her face. 'Ouch.'

'Yeah. He swore me to silence, and told me that if my mum ever found out I'd be responsible for breaking up the family.'

'Oh, a nice guy, then.' Her hand flew to her mouth. 'Sorry. He was your father…'

'Don't be. They're my sentiments exactly. It went on for years, and he used me as a smoke-screen. Used to tell my mum that he was taking me out somewhere, and he'd drop me off in the park and disappear for a couple of hours. When I got back home I'd have to say what a nice time we'd had together and Mum always used to ask exactly what we'd done, as if she had some idea that I was lying. I used to dread it.'

'That's outrageous, Joel. It's abuse.'

Joel shrugged. 'I didn't think of it like that…'

'You were being intentionally harmed by an adult. You were manipulated and threatened, and made to feel that you'd be to blame if you spoke out. I work with kids and that's one definition of abuse.'

The heat of her outrage warmed him. Joel wondered again what it might have been like if he'd had an adult like Robbie in his life. Maybe this secret didn't have as much power over him as he'd thought. Maybe Robbie would be the one that set him free.

'I just felt guilty. I had this secret that I knew would hurt my mum, and I couldn't bear to tell her. But not telling her was hard to bear, too.'

'I'm so sorry that happened to you. And I'm really sorry that you were made to feel guilty about it, because it wasn't your fault.'

She was saying all the right things. And she said them with such passion, such implacable certainty, that they struck straight into his heart. He believed her.

'Did your mum ever find out?'

That was the worst admission of all. That

he'd never put right the things he'd done as a child.

'Not from me. When I got a place at medical school I left home, and I wasn't very good at going back. It was just all too difficult, and I made an excuse not to go home at Christmas because I didn't want to see my father. My mum died suddenly the following February and…it's too late now. I didn't know how to tell her the secret, because I'd kept it for so long, and it drove us apart. It ate away at my relationships with the rest of my family too, my younger brother and my mother's sister.'

'They don't know what happened?' Her gaze held him warm and soft in its embrace. Somehow it was all right to tell Robbie.

'No. My brother doesn't understand why I've stayed away, and I haven't seen him in a long time. I pop in to see my aunt from time to time but…' Joel shrugged. 'It's hard. This is the one thing I want to talk about but can't and it's driven a wedge between us.'

'Your mother and her sister were close?'

'Very. That's what makes it so difficult. I don't want to hurt Aunt Carrie.'

Robbie thought for a moment. 'Has it occurred to you that…' She seemed suddenly at a loss, pressing her lips together tightly as if she was making up her mind whether or not to say something.

'There are probably quite a few things that haven't occurred to me. Give me a clue.'

She nodded. 'It's just that my sister and I are close, and we generally know when something's the matter before it's even said. Are you *sure* your aunt Carrie didn't know—or at least suspect that something was up?'

That hadn't occurred to Joel, but when he thought about it, it didn't seem so unlikely. 'Maybe. Perhaps it's not too late to mend some bridges with Carrie, but I can never put things right with my mother.'

Robbie reached forward, taking his hand and squeezing it tight. 'Some things aren't yours to put right, Joel. It was your parents' marriage. It doesn't matter what your mother knew or didn't know, and it makes no difference what your father wanted to cover up. You had no responsibility for anything, not to keep quiet when you were a child, or to tell your mother later on.'

It all sounded so simple when Robbie said it. 'You think that's so?'

She rolled her eyes. 'You're asking me because I'm so good at relationships? I don't know, but I do know that what your father did was very wrong, and that everything that's resulted from that is his fault and not yours. I'm not surprised you're cautious in your relationships.'

The weight was lifting from his chest, and with it Joel's need for euphemism. 'Maybe cautious doesn't cover it. That implies I actually *have* relationships.'

'You mean…' She gave him a confused look. 'I don't even know how to ask.'

She was grappling with something. Robbie had already listened to the worst thing that he could think of to say about himself, and she'd made the first time he'd spoken about it easy. There was nothing she couldn't say to him now.

He picked up her hand, bringing it to his lips. The sensation of being close to her, of being able to touch her and show her how he felt, was almost overwhelming and he could see an equal and opposite reaction in Robbie, pushing back and making him want more.

Her cheeks began to flush a little, and Joel tested their smooth heat with the tips of his fingers. Was this where he finally took the plunge, and let his feelings for someone complicate the simple satisfaction of sex?

'Does this make it any easier?'

She swallowed hard. 'Not really. Are you

telling me that you've never been with any-one before?'

Robbie had it wrong. This might be a first, but not that kind of first. 'You mean have I had sex with a woman before—'

'It doesn't matter.' She interrupted him, red-dening furiously now.

Joel couldn't help laughing and he saw a flash of indignation in her face. This was al-ready far more fun than the cool exchange be-tween two people who knew what they wanted and were sure that commitment wasn't on the list. More awkward and much more entrancing.

'Yes, I have.' He resisted the temptation to say *plenty of times* and that they'd all merged into one take-it-or-leave-it experience. 'I'm a relationships virgin, though.'

Her eyes widened and she pushed him away. Clearly that was a little more of a problem to her and Joel had to admit that he was liking the challenge. Perhaps a little more than he ought to.

'You're sure I'm the one, Joel. I work nights...' Her fingers had wandered to her neck and she was rubbing the skin. 'I don't go to bed before I've spent half an hour in the bathroom, and if my eczema does flare there are times I don't want to be touched. I'm probably not the one to get involved with as a first… And don't smile at me like that, I can't think properly.'

Good. That was exactly how he felt. Joel pulled his face straight, but he couldn't stop smiling on the inside.

'I know what having friends is like, Robbie. I have plenty of them. It's about valuing someone for what they are and reckoning that it's your privilege to compromise as much as you need to for them. About knowing what hurts them and respecting their boundaries. Knowing what pleases them.'

She stared at him, the flush mounting on her cheeks. Joel reached forward, taking her hand. 'Do I please you?'

'Yes.' She seemed certain of that, at least. 'You please me…a lot. Much more than a lot…'

'That's about how much I want to kiss you right now.'

That made her smile. She leaned forward, brushing her lips against his. This was a courtship, with all the bear traps and pitfalls and all the exquisite pleasures of finding that he *could* please her. When he kissed her back he felt a shiver run through her whole body.

'I have to…um…stop.'

The one word that would put an end to it, immediately. It wasn't as frustrating as Joel might have thought, because doing what Robbie wanted was what *he* wanted.

'Sure. We'll stop.'

Seriously. Joel thought he knew nothing about relationships? He knew everything he needed to know, which was a great deal more than she did. He leaned back on the sofa, his arm on the cushions behind her back.

'I didn't mean stop. I meant…pause.' He hadn't asked why, and Robbie was sure he wouldn't if she didn't volunteer the information. 'That half an hour I said I needed to spend in the bathroom…'

He nodded, understanding now. 'Robbie, you owned my secrets and you took them and made them something different. If I tell you that I want to be with you, it's not a tactful way of saying that I want to make love to you. I mean that I want to be with you.'

Joel was just too good to be true. Robbie hoped that wasn't a reason to disbelieve him. 'I'd like that.'

'Then will you wait for me, just for a moment while I fetch my shaver from the car? Then we can do whatever we need to do together.'

Whatever *we* need to do. There was no you or I, no impatience in his tone. And she hadn't even had to mention that beard burn wasn't a good look for her, he'd already thought of it.

'The keys are on the hook, behind the door.' She leaned forward, kissing his cheek, and Joel got to his feet. He gave her the wickedest look she'd ever seen and then he was gone before she had a chance to demand that he hurry.

Those few moments of quiet were enough to break her nerve. Robbie hurried into the bathroom, staring at her own face in the full-length mirror. What if he couldn't do this? What happened if Joel retreated into the safety of a throwaway affair and they lost the friendship that had become so important to her? What if the secret that she hadn't told yet came back to slap her in the face? Who she really was, who her family were.

'Hey...' She hadn't heard the front door open again. She must have been lost in her thoughts. Joel was standing at the bathroom door, and the sudden rush of desire swallowed everything else up.

'Second thoughts?'

'No.' There was only one thought in her head now: she wanted him to kiss her. Or just touch her.

But it seemed that Joel had other ideas. He walked into the bathroom, propping his shaver on the shelf above the basin. Then he pulled his sweater and T-shirt over his head together. Nice. She reached for him and he took a step back, grinning.

'Is this look but don't touch?' She smiled at him. 'Don't get me wrong, I'm liking what I see.' She liked it better that Joel was even doing this. That he had the confidence to stand half naked before her, without needing anything back.

'It's whatever you want it to be.'

'You should know that I'll be doing all kinds of touching in my head.'

'So will I.' The idea was clearly turning him on. 'You can tell me all about that, later.'

She turned, twisting the taps of the large bathtub. 'I like this game. Your move.'

He knew just what she wanted him to do. His shoes came off, then his jeans and socks and then his underpants. His body was beautiful, there was no doubt about that, and becoming harder by the moment as if her gaze had the power to actually touch him. He liked the game too.

Joel got into the bathtub and she perched on the rim of it, soaping her hands. Robbie could feel the muscles tighten in his shoulders as she began to wash him. Suddenly he slid forward, ducking his head beneath the water and then resurfacing with a splash.

'Can I see a little more of you?'

'Fair's fair.' Robbie wriggled out of her loose sweatshirt and T-shirt, dropping them on top of his clothes. She could unhook her bra with one hand, and the knowledge that he was watching sent tingles racing across her skin. Whatever happened next, they didn't need to stop for anything, because sex with Joel clearly wasn't something you could only do in a bed with the lights turned off. It was anything and every-thing, the practical blended with the sensual, all bound up in a growing arousal that *could* wait but might not.

They washed each other, and then Joel got out of the bath, wrapping a towel around his waist and helping her out. He carefully rubbed emollient cream into her back, stopping to gently press his thumbs on either side of her spine in a tingling massage. She shaved him, carefully, her fingers caressing his cheek as she did so.

When she led him into the bedroom, there was no question of closing the curtains because the morning sun caressed every line of his body. He sat down on the bed, and Robbie took the condoms from the drawer. When she stood between his outstretched legs he could reach every part of her body, and that was just the way she wanted it.

'Here…' He guided her hand onto his shoulder and lifted her a little so she could tuck her legs on either side of his body. Then he shifted back. 'You like this?'

'Maybe a little too much.' She kissed him. If they weren't careful it would all be over too soon.

'Is there such a thing as liking it too much?' She felt his hands tighten on her hips, stopping her from moving, and Robbie caught her breath. When he kissed her, holding her tight against his body, all she wanted was what he wanted.

He wanted a great deal. He wanted to make sure that she was ready for him, before he gently lifted her so that she could guide him inside. Sighs weren't enough, he wanted to hear her call his name. He wanted to feel her shake with passion and he wanted her to look into his gaze so that they could share each moment of it.

He made her come so hard that she cried out, and as the aftershocks were still pulsing through her body she felt him stiffen and swell inside her. One movement of her hips, and his head snapped back. She held him tight, feeling the shock waves that were travelling through his limbs.

Then he lifted her off him, his body still

shaking. Robbie curled up in a ball next to him, her legs still twitching involuntarily, and Joel flopped back onto the bed. His hand reached for hers, holding it tight. That one small contact was enough, because she knew that Joel belonged to her, and that she belonged to him.

She heard his breathing begin to steady and felt him move. He rolled onto his side to face her. 'I'm sorry… I'm not that guy that rolls over and falls asleep.'

Robbie was still trying to gather her scattered wits, but she knew one thing for sure. She laid her finger across his lips. 'Don't you *dare* say sorry, Joel. I like it that you're the guy that gave so much he needed a moment to catch his breath.'

'You felt it too?' His mouth curved into a broad grin. 'When I said I'd done this before, I didn't actually mean *this*.'

'Me neither.' This was a first for Robbie, too. Knowing that someone wanted to share everything and allowing them to do it. It had formed a bond between them that had been strong enough to contain the fiercest desire. 'Must have been something you did.'

'No. Definitely wasn't me, it must have been you.' His fingers skimmed her cheek, moving slowly down to her neck and shoulders. Robbie could feel the tingling murmur of her skin, still reacting to his touch.

And she could still feel the heat of his gaze, as their bodies slowly began to wind back down again. When she shivered, finally sensing the cool touch of the air around her, he drew back the covers of the bed, propping a pillow on one side of her to support her shoulder.

She didn't want to lie on her back, staring at the ceiling. She wanted to curl up in his arms to sleep, however stiff her shoulder might be as a result. But he hushed her protests, curling his legs under hers and taking her hand in his.

'Just sleep.' He pressed her fingers to his lips.

She was already warm and comfortable, and beginning to relax. 'We're not doing that again, Joel. Not until…this evening at least.'

She heard him chuckle quietly. 'No. Definitely not. I don't think I could take it…'

'Me neither.' Robbie's eyelids were drooping and she was half asleep now. This evening couldn't come too soon.

CHAPTER TEN

JOEL WATCHED HER sleep until the warm languor in his limbs made him unable to prop himself up on his elbow any longer. Carefully keeping hold of her hand, he curled around her in the bed as best he could without disturbing her.

So *this* was what a relationship was like. He dismissed the thought. It was what Robbie was like. Full of sweetness and strength, and there to share all the things he'd never spoken about before. Sharing her doubts and fears with him. He drifted off to sleep, wondering if he'd ever be the same and knowing that she'd already made him into a better man than the one she'd found.

One who couldn't get enough of her touch. He woke early in the afternoon, to hear rain beating against the windows. And Robbie was already awake, whispering in his ear.

'Don't move…'

'Uh? Why not?' He decided that he didn't

really care why not. If Robbie wanted him to stay still, then that was what he'd do.

If he could. Her head popped beneath the covers and he felt her lips on his chest. Desire flooded through him and he reached for her, feeling her push his hands away.

'Are you leaning on your shoulder?' He tried to focus on the practicalities and managed to get one sentence out.

'No.'

He felt her tongue circle his nipple and Joel groaned. This was just too sweet to stop her, and he clasped his hands behind his head, waiting for whatever was going to happen next. When Robbie was done with him, there would be plenty of time to return the favour...

They'd been in bed for maybe twelve hours. He'd made sure that Robbie had been resting comfortably for eight of them, and for the rest of the time they'd been talking and making love. Rather more making love than talking, because actions spoke a great deal louder than words.

But it was time to get up. The Nightshifters phones were covered until midnight, by a volunteer who worked the day shift, but they were on the rota for the following eight hours. Robbie showered and got dressed while Joel made egg-and-bacon sandwiches, and they hurried out to the car in the rain.

The sound of rain on the roof in the Tin Tabernacle was already moving from a soothing patter to a deafening roar. Ava, who had been covering the phones for the first part of the night, packed her things up and ran out through the pelting rain to her car, leaving them alone. Robbie closed the door behind her and turned, grinning at Joel.

'Don't you love the sound of the rain? When I was little we had a tree house, and when it rained it sounded just like this.'

Robbie's memories of her childhood were obviously happier than his. 'I'll take here and now. With you.'

She nodded. 'Me too. Rain on the roof is all yours from now on.'

That might be a little rash, because their relationship wasn't even twenty-four hours old yet. But rain on the roof would always be Robbie's, even if the next thing she did was walk away from him and he never saw her again.

And that wasn't going to happen. He couldn't let it happen.

Joel unwrapped the sandwiches, which were still warm inside the greaseproof paper, and made the coffee, while Robbie took a call.

Then the phone fell silent and they could tuck into their food.

'Who was that?' Robbie hadn't made any of the usual follow-up calls to find out if a driver was available.

'Glen. He won't be in tonight, the kids both have a feverish cold that's been going around at school, and Carla's caught it now as well. Probably only a matter of time before he goes down with it, but until then he's on hot lemon and cuddling duty.'

'And wondering how we're managing?'

'Yes. I told him we were fine, that you were here and he was to shut up and go away. He does enough already.'

Joel nodded. 'Yeah, I can always do a few deliveries...' He forgot all about deliveries as a crash sounded behind him followed by the sound of dribbling water. Robbie was staring up at the ceiling, her hand over her mouth, and when he turned to see what she was looking at he could see why. Water was trickling through one of the joints in the wooden panelling of the pitched ceiling and onto the floor, next to one of the sofas.

'Oh, no! We just had the roof done last year...'

'Sounds as if something's fallen on it.' Joel got to his feet, looking around. 'Do we have something to catch the water before it gets everywhere and damages the floor?'

'There are buckets in the storeroom.' Robbie opened the door behind her, disappearing into the storeroom that had everything, and reappearing with a large bucket in her hand. She placed it under the leak in the roof, while Joel looked under the sink for a cloth to wipe up the mess.

'That'll hold it for...' He glanced at the bucket, which was already beginning to fill.

'About half an hour. Tops.' Robbie sighed.

'I'll go outside and see what's happened. Torch?' There *had* to be at least a couple of torches in the storeroom.

'Yes.' Instead of fetching a torch, Robbie had reached for her waterproof jacket and was threading her arm into it. 'I'll go.'

'You will not. Keep an eye on the phones, and I'll go.'

'This is *my* place...'

That wasn't entirely true, but Robbie was clearly very attached to the Tin Tabernacle. All the same, Joel wasn't going to allow her to go out in the pouring rain to inspect the roof.

'Your shoulder is still weak, Robbie. And you're...' He thought twice about what he'd been about to say. 'We're in a relationship.'

She glared up at him. 'Oh, and because

we're in a relationship, that makes me the little woman, does it? Think again, Joel.'

She'd been *all* woman with him today and if he was totally honest that had changed his view of her slightly. Joel decided not to mention that. Robbie was already cross enough.

'No. It makes us a team. You're shorter than I am and I have greater reach, even supposing your shoulder was fully healed, which it's not. It's about each of us doing what we can do best.'

Robbie narrowed her eyes. 'That makes sense. I'm very cross with you for it, though.'

'Fine.' He grinned back at her. Robbie's fiery independence was one of her most attractive traits. 'You can watch the phone while you're being cross. And tell me where I can find a torch.'

She turned on her heel, marching back to the storeroom and fetched him a large lantern torch. Joel zipped his waterproof jacket up, pulling the hood over his head, and made for the door, turning when Robbie called him back.

'Be safe, darling.' She was smiling, waving a paper handkerchief from the box on her desk. Joel started to laugh, and she poked her tongue out at him.

'Just do a little light dusting with that hanky…

While I'm gone.' He turned before Robbie could throw something at him, making his way outside to the relative safety of the storm.

Wonderful. Robbie looked at her watch. Sixteen hours in, and she'd already allowed her fears to get the better of her judgement.

Of course, Joel was taller and stronger than she was. Of course, she wasn't going to be much use, when her arm still protested when she lifted it above shoulder level, or put any weight on it. And how was he to know that the Tin Tabernacle really was hers and she'd put her heart into renovating it, if she'd never told him?

But she'd reacted to the situation with all of the hurt that she'd felt when she was with Rory. He'd seen only that she was weak and flawed, and had decided that making her dependent on him was a project that carried some financial reward. He'd crushed her confidence, and she'd fought back by deciding that she could do anything. Mending a broken roof in the rain was nothing...

She stared at the phone, almost willing it to ring so that she could prove to herself that she could do something useful. That was ridiculous. Joel had never said she was useless, and she knew that wasn't what he thought, either.

There was a rattling at the door and it opened. 'I'm sorry...' The apology died in her throat when she saw that it wasn't Joel. Clara and Joan were both shrouded in knee-length waterproof jackets, which were dripping onto the floor.

'Come in. Close the door.' Robbie got to her feet. 'Are you okay?'

'Yeah, we're fine.' Clara pulled down her hood, her mass of red hair spilling out over her shoulders. 'We've pulled the tarps over the front and rear decks on the barge and slackened off the mooring ropes, so she'll be fine. But she's rocking like Elvis.'

'Well, make yourselves at home. You might not get much sleep here with the phone ringing, but it's warm and dry.'

Joan smiled, taking off her jacket to reveal a thick multicoloured sweater. 'Thanks. Being at the same angle for more than five seconds is a huge improvement.'

Clara had caught sight of the bucket. 'Roof leaking?'

'Yes, it's only just started. Joel's out there trying to see what the matter is. We might be able to fix it from the inside.'

Clara and Joan both looked up at the ceiling. People here were used to making and mending and the small, self-sufficient community was one of the things that had first drawn Robbie here.

'Yeah, I reckon you probably could. Can you remove the wooden cladding?' Clara gave her verdict on the situation.

'Yes, it's designed so that the panels will slide out, so we can get to the roof from the inside. Specifically with leaks in mind. The old roof leaked like a sieve. We've got some sealant and stuff to patch it with in the storeroom.'

A creaking sound came from the roof and then a sharp bang. All three women stared up at it. Then the leak slowed.

'It looks as if he's done something.'

'Yeah.' Clara walked over to the bucket, her gaze fixed on the ceiling. 'It's definitely not dripping so fast now.'

The roof creaked and another, louder bang made Robbie jump, clutching at her shoulder as she did so in an instinctive expectation of pain. Then she forgot all about the slight tremor that ran down her arm, because the dripping slowed again and then stopped.

Clara gave a nod of approval. 'He's done it.'

When Joel appeared in the doorway, wet and windblown, Robbie had to stop herself from running over to him and hugging him.

'How's it looking now?' He pulled back his

hood and saw Joan and Clara. 'Hi there. Everything all right?'

'Yes, it's just a bit choppy out there,' Joan answered and he nodded.

'And the drip's stopped.' Robbie grinned at him. 'What did you do?'

'There was a branch lodged between two of the corrugated panels. It's pretty windy out there and it must have blown up against the roof. I pulled it out and then climbed up and gave the top panel a thump and they snapped back together again.'

Robbie decided not to ask him how he'd managed to climb up onto the roof in the pouring rain. It probably wasn't all that difficult—he could have stood on the windowsill and levered himself up from there.

'Thank you. I'll get someone out to have a look at it in the morning, but at least it's stopped for now.'

His smile was just for her. But when he strode towards her, Robbie turned her face away from him before he could kiss her, aware that Clara's and Joan's eyes were on them.

His mouth twitched downwards, but he gave an imperceptible nod and stopped at a respectful distance away from her. No one owned up to a relationship this new, did they? Didn't keeping that secret for a little while just add to the heady excitement of it all?

Not for Joel. He'd been hurt by secrets, and he probably didn't find keeping this secret quite as deliciously exciting as she did. She grabbed his hand, pulling him close.

Are you sure? He mouthed the words at her. It was a bit late for that now—what she'd done could hardly have escaped Joan and Clara's notice. And she didn't want it to.

She stood on her toes, kissing him. Maybe that would show him how sure she was. How she could leave her own doubts and fears and need to be in control behind, in favour of making him feel more comfortable. Although she knew there were still things she needed to tell him…

As he drew away from her he was smiling. He mouthed *Thank you* and then turned away, but not before Robbie had caught an exchanged glance between Clara and Joan. By morning, the news would probably have reached everyone in their small community, but Robbie couldn't bring herself to care.

'The boat a little further up, painted red and green. That's Roy's, isn't it?' Joel's smile still lingered, but there was a note of concern in his voice now.

'Yes?'

'It's just that all the other boats have covers at the back and front, but he hasn't pulled his across. Should we go and wake him?'

'I can't imagine anyone hasn't been woken by this storm. And it's not like Roy, he's usually the first to keep his boat protected from the weather…' Robbie glanced round at Clara, who gave her an innocent look, as if she really hadn't been watching every move that she and Joel made.

'Have you seen Roy? Joel says he hasn't covered his front and rear decks.'

'No. Come to think of it I haven't seen him all day. Is he on the boat, Joan?'

Joan shrugged. 'He didn't say anything to me about going away, and he usually does, so we can keep an eye on his boat.'

'We'd better check on him.' Robbie glanced up at Joel. 'It'll only take five minutes. We can put the answerphone on.'

'I'll answer the phones. I've always rather fancied being a Nightshifter,' Clara volunteered, and Joel gave her a smile.

'That's great, thanks. Just a name and number is fine, but if you can find out what they need and write that down that'll be great. If it's one of the drivers, then tell them they can come back here, we've no outstanding calls.'

'Gotcha. Can I sit at your desk, Robbie?'

'Of course. There's a packet of fruit gums in the top drawer.' Robbie eased on her jacket, and followed Joel out into the pouring rain.

The towpath was illuminated by a string of bright streetlights, but Roy's narrowboat was in darkness. Joel switched on the torch, and Robbie saw dark shapes of furniture and seating inside as the beam of light played across the windows.

'This isn't right, Joel. He hasn't even closed his curtains.'

'I don't see anyone in there. Where's the bedroom?'

'It'll be near the back.' Robbie walked along the towpath to the approximate place. 'About here.'

Joel shone the light at the windows again, bending down to get a better view. Robbie could see the shape of what looked like a man, on what looked like a bed.

'I can't see properly. But this isn't right, Joel. We should go inside and check on him.'

He nodded, hurrying back to the bow of the boat and stepping across onto the small deck. Reaching back, he coiled his arm around her waist, almost lifting her over the gap between the towpath and the boat. Then he turned, banging on the door and calling Roy's name.

Nothing. No lights, no answer. Joel started

to look around the deck, obviously trying to find something to force the door. That might not be necessary. Robbie gave it a push and it slid open.

'Really?' He stepped inside, looking around him.

'People often don't lock their doors during the day, when they're up and around.' Robbie shoved the door closed behind them with her foot then slid her hand along the wall and found the light switch.

Nothing. She flipped the switch on and off a couple of times, to make sure.

'The boat's batteries must be drained, Joel. There's no light.'

He nodded, calling out again, and this time there was a reply, an indistinct but agonised mumble of words. The lights outside were reflecting into the boat and were just enough to see their way forward. Robbie followed Joel, stumbling as the boat rocked in response to a gust of wind outside, and feeling his arm around her waist before she could fall.

'I've got you.'

The words might be possessive and protective and all the other things that she'd rejected over the years. But Joel turned them into the fierce heat that she'd seen in his eyes when they were making love, and she couldn't forget that he'd revelled in *her* possessiveness, her protective instincts too.

'Yes. You have.' She murmured the words as they moved forward, Joel's arm around her to steady her.

Through the sitting area into a well-equipped kitchen, and then past that into a study, the books held in place by rails across the front of the shelves. The narrowboats afforded a surprisingly big living area once you were inside, and the unsteady rocking motion meant they had to take care, but finally Joel slid back the door to the bedroom. In the half-light all Robbie could see was a shrouded figure on the bed, and a hand raised against the beam of the torch. She hung onto the door frame, while Joel moved forward towards the bed, making sure to keep the beam of the torch from shining directly at its occupant.

'Hey, Roy. It's Joel and Robbie, we've come to see if you're okay.'

'Feeling pretty groggy...' The sound of Roy's voice attested to that better than his words, and the disorder and stale scent of the cabin was a world away from his usually spotless narrowboat.

'Okay. How long for?'

'This morning...'

'And what's the matter?' Joel laid his hand

on Roy's forehead to check for a fever, and then his fingers felt for the pulse in his neck. Crude measurements, but that was all he had right now.

'Legs hurt…everything hurts. Can't keep any food down… Thank goodness you're here…'

Roy was as self-sufficient as anyone living on this stretch of the river. If he could move, he would be doing so and would probably have made his way up to the Tin Tabernacle with the others, and be drinking peppermint tea to calm his stomach. Joel glanced over his shoulder at Robbie and she shook her head.

'This isn't like him. He's really sick.'

'Roy, I'm going to have to just check you over to see if I can find out what the matter is.' He reached for the torch and Roy caught his arm.

'My head hurts…'

'Okay. I hear you. But I need to be able to see a little more. I'll shine the torch away from your face.'

Joel tried to calm him, checking his head for any bumps or bleeding as he did so, but the boat lurched again and he only just managed to snatch his hands away from Roy before he slid back against the cupboards lining the other side of the narrow cabin. This wasn't going to work.

'Joel, we need to get him out so that we can see what the matter is. There's a basket stretcher in the storeroom, go and fetch that and find someone to help you. Chloe and Grant are two boats along from here, see if you can find Grant. I'll stay here with Roy.'

If Joel was thinking of arguing, he dismissed the idea quickly. Getting to his feet, he helped her to the low cabinet beside the bed, clearing the top of it so she had somewhere to sit securely.

'Okay, hang on. I'll be back as soon as I can. You've got your phone?'

'Yes, I'll call you if he takes a turn for the worse.'

There wasn't much that Robbie could do here, other than to use what movement she had in her shoulder to try and check Roy's breathing and heartbeat, while she hung on with the other hand. But the sound of her voice seemed to soothe Roy and she kept talking, telling him Joel would be back shortly and that he'd be more comfortable when they got him up to the Tin Tabernacle. Sooner than she'd even dared to hope, she heard voices outside and the sound of someone boarding the boat again.

Stretching forward, she could see along the whole length of the boat. Joel was coming towards them, struggling to stay on his feet and

manage the stretcher and behind him Grant
was carrying the vinyl-covered insert and a
couple of blankets.

Leaving the stretcher in the doorway to the
bedroom, Joel wedged himself in next to Robbie at the side of the bed. 'How is he?'

'Low-grade fever, pulse seems steady. I can't
find any bleeding and his breathing seems
okay.' Robbie shook her head silently, and Joel
got the message. It was impossible to tell exactly what was going on in these conditions,
and Roy was clearly very unwell.

'We'll move him?'

'Yes, we'll move him.'

'Out of the way, then.'

Robbie squeezed past him, finding yet another reason to be grateful that last night had
happened. If it hadn't Joel might have thought
twice about putting his hands where they were
resting right now, and it was actually the best
way to stop her from falling over.

'Grant, will you put the vinyl insert into
the stretcher…?' She helped Grant prepare
the stretcher while Joel carefully sat Roy up
on the bed.

'That's great. Now we'll slide it forwards
towards Joel.'

What might have been a desperate, fumbling
exercise turned into a well-executed manoeu-

vre. Joel helped Roy to swing his legs over the side of the bed, and carefully supported him down into the stretcher tucking the blankets and then a waterproof sheet over him, and fastening the straps around him.

Robbie went first, the torch tucked into the crook of her elbow, to leave her other arm free for the handholds along the way. The men followed, with the stretcher steering it carefully behind her to the front of the boat. When she reached the sliding door at the other end of the boat, she pushed it back with her foot, moving out onto the small deck.

Willing hands grabbed her, bearing her off the boat. A small crowd had gathered on the towpath, standing in the pouring rain, waiting for news of Roy. That was both good and bad.

'All right—everyone stand back, please, give us some room. Chloe, will you go on board, please, and give Joel and Grant a hand? Ollie and Rachel, would you come and wait with me? They'll be passing the stretcher off the boat and as soon as you can reach it you grab hold of it.' Robbie looked around and saw that Joel was already beginning to manoeuvre the stretcher round. 'Great. Perfect. Anyone got an umbrella I can borrow?'

She took the closest of three umbrellas that were offered, and turned to find Rachel leaning forward, almost climbing onto the boat in her eagerness to help. Robbie took her arm, guiding her back. 'It's okay, we need to have a safe footing up here on the towpath. They'll pass the stretcher over to you and you take it when you can reach it.'

'Ready?' Joel called across to her, and Robbie gave him a thumbs-up. The stretcher was passed smoothly and easily onto the towpath, Joel stepping across with it. Robbie shielded Roy's face from the rain as best she could with the umbrella, as they walked across the towpath and up to the Tin Tabernacle.

Inside, there was the evidence of activity as well. Geoff, one of the Nightshifters, had returned and was monitoring the phones and Joan and Clara had clearly been busy moving furniture. The desks had been pulled forward, and an old curtain draped from the rafters, to provide a space next to the storeroom that afforded some measure of privacy. The dozen or so people who followed them into the Tin Tabernacle formed a tight group at the other end of the office, talking amongst themselves in hushed tones.

Joel grinned at her as he set the stretcher down on the floor and took off his jacket. One hand briefly went to his heart and Robbie nodded. This community could be rambunctious and argumentative and the reason many of them lived here was that they didn't much like doing as they were told, but the care they showed to one of their own when they were hurt was touching.

He undid the straps that secured Roy into the stretcher and Chloe and Grant helped him get Roy onto the camp bed that had been set up ready for them, while Robbie shrugged out of her jacket and fetched the medical kit from the storeroom. Roy was moaning, shading his eyes as if the light hurt them.

'Roy, we need the light to examine you. Just close your eyes, and try to relax. We'll let you know what's happening.' Robbie knelt down beside the bed and Joel opened the medical kit, squirting a dab of hand sanitiser onto his hands and then another onto Robbie's outstretched palm. Then he grabbed two pairs of surgical gloves, holding hers open for her to slide her hands into, before putting on a pair himself.

'I'll do the history—you do the exam?' She grinned up at him.

'Yep.' He popped his head around the side of the curtain asking for a pen and paper, and Robbie took them, ready to write everything down.

It was a lot quicker with two, working together without getting in each other's way. Roy had been suffering from vomiting and abdominal pain for the last six hours, along with severe muscle aches, a headache and a fever. When Joel uncovered his feet, there were the telltale signs of a rash.

Joel glanced at Robbie and she nodded. They didn't need to discuss what he should check next. 'Roy, I'm going to need you to open your eyes for a moment, so I can take a look at them.'

Roy shook his head, and Robbie cupped her hand on his forehead. 'I'm shading your eyes. But you have to open them just for a moment.'

Roy opened his eyes, blinking against the light. It took one look to confirm what Robbie had been thinking and Joel clearly didn't need any more than that either.

They left Roy to rest, walking a few steps to the corner of their makeshift booth. Each of them opened their mouths at the same time, and Joel smiled.

'After you.'

'I reckon the first stage of leptospirosis. He has most of the symptoms and the rash suggests it as well. And the conjunctival redness and jaundice…' They'd both seen the whites of Roy's eyes, and the yellow and red splotches were characteristic of leptospirosis.

Joel nodded. 'I agree. I'd say it's a mild case,

he's a little dehydrated but no more than you'd expect from having been sick, so he doesn't need intravenous fluids. And he's definitely not in the second stage yet.'

If leptospirosis didn't resolve on its own, the second stage was Weil's disease, which was much more serious. But they'd caught it early and Robbie was confident that with a course of antibiotics to prevent the onset of the second stage, Roy would be feeling much better soon.

Joel didn't seem as happy about it all as she was. 'Normally I'd take a blood sample to confirm our diagnosis, and prescribe antibiotics and rest. But we can't just let him back onto the boat. He needs someone to keep an eye on him.'

'He has someone.' Robbie smiled at Joel's expression of surprise. 'Roy has a really big house about ten minutes' walk from here. His daughter and son-in-law live in one side of it, and Roy mostly lives on the boat, but he pops in and out of his side of the house whenever the mood takes him.'

'Ah. So if we call the daughter...?'

'She'll take good care of him. They're really close and I've met her, she seems sensible. We've got blood-sampling kits here, so we can do that now.'

'And I can take the blood sample straight to the hospital and write a prescription while I'm there. Do we know who his GP is?'

'Yes, it's one of the doctors who comes here twice a week. I can give him a call in the morning.'

'That's everything sorted, then.' Joel jerked his thumb towards the curtain. 'I'm rather hoping you might know what to say to the assembled well-wishers…'

Robbie chuckled. 'I'll say what we'd say if they all turned up with him in A & E. We expect him to make a full recovery, and he should be back on the boat soon. If someone wants to go and sit with him, that would be nice, but they're to keep quiet.'

'Rather you than me.' Joel didn't seem entirely confident that just saying no if anyone asked for more details would work. 'Do you have any idea how he got it?'

'Well, it's a waterborne infection. Most people here know how to avoid it and our clinics always emphasise the need for precautions, even if it's not likely you'll get it just living on the water. I'll see if I can find out a bit more while you're at the hospital. Roy may have fallen in and got a mouthful of the Thames at some point.'

'Okay.' He smiled at her, taking her hand. 'You go and talk to the assembled neighbours, and I'll do the easy part and take some blood.'

CHAPTER ELEVEN

IT WAS NINE in the morning. They should be gone by now, but Joel and Robbie were taking advantage of a few moments' peace, and were sitting back in the two office chairs, their feet on the desks, sipping coffee.

'So… marine rescue.'

Joel gave her a pained look. 'Can you really call it that? We were within a few metres of the towpath at all times.'

'On the water is on the water. Ask anyone here.'

'Okay. In that case breaking and entering.'

Robbie chuckled. 'No, I'm not going to give you that, the door was open. Diagnosis, treatment and family liaison.' Roy's daughter Kirsty had come to collect her father at six this morning, and while he was sleeping Joel had taken her through exactly what was needed and which symptoms she should look out for.

'Yep. Howling winds and a roof repair.'

Robbie looked up at the wooden ceiling cladding, which was drying out nicely. 'Yes, and I'd like to compliment you on the effectiveness of your repairs.'

'Thank you. Public health education because Chloe was really worried about having dangled her feet in the water three weeks ago. And then several hours on the phones with Nightshifters. That counts as two, by the way.'

'Absolutely. Although Clara made a fine job of covering while you were at the hospital and I was sitting with Roy. She said that once you've got someone to measure their five-year-old for a sweater, over the phone, this was a piece of cake.'

Joel grinned. 'Did you mention that you could do with a few more volunteers?'

'Yes, I did actually. She said she quite enjoyed being involved, and she's thinking about it. As long as she can bring her knitting with her.'

'Then that's recruitment as well. Have we got everything?'

'I think so.' Robbie thought through the events of the night and decided that it was more than enough to prove her point. 'So since we've done all of those things since we were first together, I think we can classify ourselves as *going steady*.'

The look on his face told her that he didn't mind that at all. 'Yes. I think we can.'

'Oh, and Clara asked me if you'd like a jumper. She and Joan do these random jumpers from all the leftover wool, and they're great. I said thanks but no.'

'You're managing my wardrobe now?' Joel raised his eyebrows. 'Feel free, it could definitely do with it, and it's a pretty sure sign of going steady.'

'No, neither of us are managing each other's wardrobes.' Robbie had had quite enough of that with Rory and her relationship with Joel was different. 'It was a nice thought, and meant as an acknowledgement that you're one of us now, but I happened to mention that they hadn't knitted *me* a jumper and Clara said she'd do a matching one for me. We'd have to wear them, and we'd never live it down with the Nightshifters.'

'Sensible. Yeah, that was a good call. Matching jumpers is a step too far.' His eyes softened suddenly. 'You don't mind that they know about us?'

It had obviously been important to Joel, and although Robbie had had her reservations, she was glad she'd put them aside. 'No, I don't mind. Although, maybe we'll keep quiet about it at the hospital for a little while.'

He chuckled. 'That's definitely a good idea. We don't need to run round telling absolutely everyone. It was just a really nice gesture of yours to tell people that you care about. I'm assuming that everyone probably knows by now?'

'Roy might have missed it, but only because he wasn't feeling well.' Robbie smiled at him. 'I suppose this all makes it quite all right to say, *Your place or mine?*'

His smile broadened. 'That would be more than all right. And although I'd love to say mine, I think I have laundry and shopping to do first. That's as long as it's not too presumptuous of me to hope that you may consider coming in contact with my sheets and my soap.'

'I was planning on getting you in contact with my sheets at the earliest possible opportunity. So no, it's not presumptuous at all. And if you'd like to go back to yours we could always swing past my flat first and I'll get sheets and whatever else I need.'

'Do you mind?'

That was what was so refreshing about Joel. He considered that if he was asking her to his home, it was his responsibility to make sure that his sheets were washed in detergent that wouldn't affect her skin, and that he had the right soap in his bathroom cabinet. It was the ultimate in gracious hosting, and made his house the most luxurious place on earth. Rory would never have understood that.

'I love that you don't mind if I bring my own things. And that you thought of it before I had to say it.'

He smiled at her, and suddenly everything was rosier than the most flamboyant sunset. 'Are you ready to go, then?'

Robbie looked around. The storm had abated at four in the morning, but everyone had stayed to tidy up and see Roy safely off before they went back to their boats, and the Tin Tabernacle showed no sign of all that had happened that night.

'Yes. I'm ready.'

They'd been together a week, and still the lustrous sheen that accompanied something new and precious hadn't dulled. Robbie was beginning to feel that it was made of strong stuff and that maybe it would never completely disappear.

'What do you think about switching to the day shift?' They were lying on his bed, watching the sun come up, when Joel asked the question. Robbie raised her eyebrows.

'Days? But we're Nightshifters, aren't we?'

In more ways than just being *actual* Nightshifters. They both enjoyed the rush of working nights. The city at night. Working in their own little bubble when everyone else was sleeping.

'We are. But we're not vampires, we won't fry if we go out in the sun.'

'I go out in the sun all the time—it's important to get your Vitamin D. And sunshine's good for the skin and helps boost your dopamine and serotonin levels. I probably get more sun than most people in the winter, because I get home from work and the sun's just coming up.'

'That's true. But right now, I just want to get up and go out and enjoy the day.' He raised her hand to his lips, kissing her fingers. 'Or maybe make love with you one more time. Then go out and enjoy the day.'

'You could make love with me one more time. I'd like that.'

Joel chuckled, rolling over onto his side, and propping himself up on one elbow.

'Your wish is my command. Particularly when you have such nice wishes.' He ran his fingers from her neck, down between her breasts and had reached her stomach before Robbie caught his hand, stopping it from going any further.

'Let's not be those people. The ones who stop talking about things because we want to have sex.'

'You don't want to have sex?' He shot her a look of exaggerated dismay. 'I'm crushed.'

'You can un-crush yourself right now, Joel. You know full well how much I love having sex with you. I also want to know why you think it's a good idea to switch to the day shift.'

He smiled. 'I just think that people work nights for lots of different reasons, because it's better paid or more convenient…whatever. But you get paid more for working unsocial hours because that's what they are. Unsocial.'

'You think we're unsocial?'

'For me, working nights was always a great excuse to keep my relationships casual, so… yeah, that's pretty unsocial. There's an awful lot to be said for working at night, and I know there's always a need for it in A & E departments. I'm just wondering whether days aren't an option as well. Better CPD opportunities, more contact with specialists who work days.'

Robbie thought for a moment. 'I suppose… I started working nights when my confidence was at a really low ebb and I just wanted to disappear.'

He grinned, leaning over to kiss her. 'How's

your confidence now? Anything I can do to boost it?'

She pushed him over onto his back, shifting to prop herself up against his chest. 'Like I said. We're not people who stop talking about things in order to have sex.'

'No. We aren't. So what do you think?'

'You've made a really good point, we both started working nights for lots of different reasons, but some of those reasons have changed now. We could think about changing with them. Only—we'd have to do it together. If I'm working days and you're working nights we'd never see each other.'

'Yeah, we'd do it together. And we can't stop working with Nightshifters, either.'

'No, but Nightshifters needs volunteers for the evenings just as much as for the early mornings. More probably. And there's a move to expand as well. The board's been scouting out a few places around Oxford.'

Robbie bit her lip. That was substantially true—her father had been doing most of the preparatory work for that, and he was on the board. 'There's something I should tell you, Joel...'

'That you're going to be involved with the expansion? That's great, you should take on more responsibility for the running of the place.' He grinned at her.

'No...well, yes and...'

His fingers were running down her back, making those patterns of sensation that she loved so much. Robbie shivered. She couldn't help it, she was going to be one of those people and put off talking about something important in order to have sex. Maybe that was the right thing to do, because she was still getting used to feeling warm and safe in Joel's arms. A little warmer, a little safer, couldn't be a bad thing when she took the step of sharing those last secrets, that had protected her for so long.

'We'll talk about the details later?'

He nodded, rolling her over onto her back and kissing her. 'Yes. Later...'

Plans. He had plans. *They* had plans, things like going away for the weekend, and seeing friends for dinner. Robbie had talked about a weekend in Ireland to meet her sister and brother-in-law, which everyone knew was a preamble to meeting her parents. Joel was unable to reciprocate on that score, but Robbie knew why and she understood.

It all felt tantalisingly normal, as if he was finally starting to leave all the guilt behind. Robbie had gently suggested that going to see

Aunt Carrie might be a good idea, just to open the channels of communication between them, and Joel was seriously considering it. It wasn't simply that Robbie had given him a new perspective on things—being with her had given him the desire to change.

Two weeks. That was all it had taken. His life had been turned upside down, and he was happier than he'd ever been.

Robbie had told him on Saturday morning that she'd be cooking and had gone home to make a start while Joel had stayed behind to follow through on a patient. When he arrived at her apartment and she buzzed him up, the kitchen was already in complete chaos.

'What are you cooking?' It was impossible to tell from the assortment of kitchen equipment spread across the worktops.

'Pizza. I've got a quick and easy recipe from Carla. And garlic bread and salad…'

'Right.' He could see a salad spinner, and it seemed to have something in it. 'Want a hand?'

'No, I'm cooking for you. You cooked for me last Saturday.'

Roast chicken with all the trimmings hadn't been quite as much trouble as this obviously was. But Robbie had a large and efficient dishwasher and cooking always made her happy, whatever the results, so he wasn't going to argue.

'Right then. Anything else you want me to do?'

'No! This is off-duty night. We eat, we talk we make love.' She grinned at him.

'Sounds good. In that order?'

She walked across the kitchen, kissing him. 'Yes. There's something I want to talk with you about, but I've got to… Oh!'

The kitchen timer pinged and she looked around. 'I'm not sure what that's for. I'll have to consult Carla's list.'

'I'll leave you to it.' Robbie seemed a little on edge tonight, and it was probably best to let her get on without interference.

'Yes, please do.' She was scanning a piece of paper that was held to the door of the fridge by a magnet. 'Prove the dough. I'm already doing that. By the way, I looked out my thesis from medical school, the one we were talking about the other day about kids in A & E. It's in the snug. In a blue binder to the right of the fireplace…'

'Okay, thanks. I'll take a look.' Robbie's work on her thesis was undoubtedly measured and perceptive, just like everything else she did medically. Cooking provided her with the opportunity to indulge in a bit of chaos, and it fed her soul in a different way. Joel was well aware of the fact that showing him these out-of-control moments was a sign of how far they'd come together in the last two weeks.

He walked into the book-lined snug, scanning the bookcases that occupied the deep alcove to the right of the fireplace. There were three or four blue binders, on two different shelves, and he pulled the nearest one out, opening it.

It was a photograph album. There were pictures of two little girls, on a beach somewhere, one of them unmistakeably Robbie. He smiled, wanting to see more but resisted the temptation to turn the page and put the album back onto the shelf.

The next blue binder had photographs in it as well, a slightly older Robbie who was just as entrancing. As he closed the cover, something fluttered from between the pages onto the floor. It was a newspaper cutting and when he picked it up, Joel couldn't help but see the headline.

Everything was under control. More or less. The pizza dough was proving and the toppings were prepared. Robbie had put everything she didn't need back into the cupboards, and she might pour herself a glass of wine before going on to the next stage.

Tonight was going to be the night. She'd suggested going to see her sister and brother-in-law, to give herself a deadline for telling Joel about her family. She was going to come clean, and tell Joel that Nightshifters was her brainchild, and that it was in the main funded by money from her trust fund. She'd tell him that the plans to expand to Oxford were already under way, and…

He'd be excited. It was something they could share and look forward to together. The little quiver of uncertainty in her stomach was just her old fears coming back to haunt her. Joel didn't care two hoots about the money, she knew that. But she'd kept it from him. Kept her family's money from him.

She saw him in the doorway, standing very still. 'Hey, did you find it? I was just about to open a bottle of wine.'

'I'm really sorry, Robbie. I was looking for the blue binder but ended up with a photo album instead.'

'Ah… No, my thesis is on the next shelf up from the albums. Same kind of binder but it's got pocket inserts instead of photo pages…' Suddenly she froze, because he was holding a newspaper cutting in his hand. *That* news-paper cutting.

It was okay. Everything was going to be okay. She'd been going to tell him anyway and she might even have shown him the newspaper cutting, even if she hated it for all the agonies of embarrassment it had caused her. But there was something about the look on Joel's face that said everything *wasn't* okay.

'I didn't mean to look at your photographs, but when I closed the album this fell out. I couldn't help seeing it and… I don't under-stand.' He laid the cutting down on the counter.

'That was what I wanted to talk to you about. It wasn't just my grandparents who had some money and left me this place. My dad's rich as well.'

Joel nodded. 'I've heard of him. David Hampton-Hall. And you're Olivia Hampton-Hall.'

'Yes, that's right. Roberta's my middle name…' A lot of people shortened a double-barrelled name or used middle names. Rob-bie felt herself blush because that hadn't been the reason. She'd deliberately tried to distance herself from the public image.

'And Nightshifters. Is that one of your fa-ther's charities?'

'No, it's *mine*. I saw the need, and I set it up

from my trust-fund money. Dad's on the board of trustees, but I asked him to help because he has a lot of experience in running a charity and I wanted his advice. There's always been an understanding between us that Nightshifters is my responsibility.' Her father had told her that he was proud of the way she'd built Nightshifters and that had meant a great deal to Robbie.

'So Glen's not really the boss, is he? It's you.'

'Yes, he is the boss. North London Nightshifters is his, and when I'm working there I do what he tells me. My side of things is... I facilitate. I make sure that Nightshifters has the financing it needs, and I'll be dealing with our plans to expand.' Robbie heaved a sigh. This wasn't going as well as she'd hoped.

'And you're on the board of trustees. Along with your father.'

'What? Well...yes, every registered charity has to have a board of trustees, and I appointed people who could help steer Nightshifters in the right direction. There's my father, a couple of his contacts from the charity sector, and a solicitor to help us with any legal issues. What does that matter, Joel?'

He was so still. His face impassive as if he wasn't feeling anything. She wanted to hug him, or shake him, or anything that would provoke a reaction.

'It matters because you lied to me. About something I was getting involved with, and which I'd started to really care about.'

'No. I didn't lie. I just didn't tell you. I have no clue what your father does for a living or who he is, because you haven't told me. I don't know your brother's name and I dare say I won't be introduced to him any time soon. I accept that, Joel, because it's your family and it's up to you what you tell me.'

'That's not the same, Robbie.' A flicker of anger showed in his face. Robbie was almost relieved to see it because at least it was something. 'I can't know everything about you, and you can't know everything about me. But you deliberately withheld information that you thought would make some difference to how I felt. You acted with purpose.'

'That's not true.' Okay, so it was a bit true. But Robbie was feeling more than a little defensive now. He was standing in her kitchen accusing her of things and he just wouldn't listen to what she was saying to him.

'All right.' She held her hands up. 'Yes, okay, there were things I withheld, and I did it deliberately. The guy I told you about, Rory, who almost ground my self-confidence into dust, do you know why he stayed? He stayed because of the money, and what he thought it could do for him. He never wanted me and…'

Robbie took a breath, trying to still the panic in her chest. 'I was afraid, Joel. The secret was my way of protecting myself from all of that, and I just didn't want to let go of it.'

'And you think I care about the money?'

'No, I don't. I *know* you don't care about it, and that was why I was going to tell you. After we'd had pizza.'

His gaze searched her face. 'Yeah, I believe you.'

'Well, thank you for that. I'm so thrilled and happy that you believe me because it's the truth.' Robbie rolled her eyes.

'But… It doesn't make any difference. You still kept it a secret. You didn't tell me the whole truth. I… I can't do this, Robbie.'

'Why not? Because I happen to have money that you don't even care about?'

Suddenly his lip curled. She'd got through to him but all she could see in his face was anger now.

'No, it's because I know all about other people's secrets and how they can twist your life. How many people know about your family at the hospital? Your father's a prominent advocate for a lot of different medical charities, I expect most people there have heard of him and some might have even met him. Has it ever come up in conversation that he happens to be related to you?'

'No one, okay? It's my business.'

'No, it's your secret and you were going to ask me to keep it. What about Nightshifters? Who apart from Glen knows that you fund the place.'

'No one.'

'So that's another secret you wanted me to keep for you.' Anger was bursting from him now. 'I'm sorry, Robbie, I know why you did it. But I can't do this for you. It's the one thing I can't do for anyone. Didn't that ever occur to you?'

'And doesn't it occur to you that the person you need to say this to is your father? Not me. I just happen to be standing in the way of all the anger you're carrying around.'

'Can't you even see what you're doing? You're trying to control everything and everyone around you, by giving them half-truths. I can't do it with you, Robbie. I'm sorry but I can't.'

She turned her back on him, so that he couldn't see the tears. 'Stop saying you're sorry, will you? Because I really don't think you are. You're just trying to hurt me because you're angry.'

Silence. She heard his footsteps and then jumped as she heard the door slam. Robbie ran out into the hallway, not knowing whether to be angry or dismayed. His coat was gone and so was the bag he usually brought up from the car, with a change of clothes and his shaving bag. She got as far as the front door and then stopped. If he was still outside, waiting for the lift, what was she going to say to him?

They were both too damaged. She'd tried to step out of the shadow of her own fears, to strip away the protective secrets, but she'd done too little, too late and she'd hurt Joel. And now he was hurting her, because he couldn't let go of his own guilt and pain over having to keep a secret.

She wouldn't cry yet. Robbie couldn't cry, because that would mean that it was really, truly over. She'd picked up her courier bag and walked from her crashed bike, hoping to find safety, and she'd found Joel. Now she had to find a different safety, and for the life of her Robbie didn't know how she was going to do that.

CHAPTER TWELVE

'Hey. You okay?'

Glen was alone at the Tin Tabernacle when Robbie arrived that evening and it was the first question that he asked. And it was the wrong question, because she really wasn't okay.

'Just a bit tired, I didn't sleep much today.'

Glen nodded. He had two kids. He knew all about not sleeping much. 'I heard about Joel.'

Tight pain gripped at her heart. She'd been hoping against hope that Joel would walk into the Tin Tabernacle tonight, as if nothing had happened. But something *had* happened, and it was impossible that life would just go on in the same way.

Robbie didn't need to go through all the palaver of keeping her shoulder quite still while she shrugged off her jacket any more, but she did it anyway because it hid her tears.

'What about Joel?'

'He called me, a couple of hours ago, and

said he can't make it in this weekend. Whatever's come up, I reckon it must be pretty big, because he doesn't know when he'll be back.'

It would have been very easy to take that sentence and pick the one strand of false optimism from it. Not knowing when he'd be back implied that he might be. Or even that he was intending to be.

'What did he say exactly?' Robbie tried to hide the quiver in her voice.

'Not for the foreseeable future.'

That was more like it. Joel couldn't foresee a time when they'd be able to work things out enough to even be in the same room. Robbie wasn't sure she could either.

She took a breath. 'Shame. We can do with all the volunteers we can get.'

'Yeah.' Glen was eyeing her thoughtfully. 'I'd assumed that you would know all about what was going on with him. Since you two are an item.'

Robbie was busying herself with the coffee machine now, making two cups. That was the problem with telling people about a new relationship—when it went wrong everyone knew it.

'Sometimes it's difficult to know exactly what Joel's thinking. He keeps things close to his chest.'

'Hmm. I might give him a call during the week. Just to see what's going on with him.'

'Maybe you should leave it.'

'Yeah, okay.' Glen always made sure that anyone on the Nightshifters team who was going through a hard time was supported, and that was the glue that held them all together, but he was taking her word on it this time. Robbie put his mug of coffee down in front of him, and sat down at the other desk.

'The phones are quiet?'

'We had a busy patch an hour ago and everyone's out. Since then, nothing.' Glen took a sip of his coffee. 'So am I going to have to put a rumour around? Something to the effect that you two have changed shifts?'

Robbie puffed out a breath. Changing shifts just about summed it up, because it was unlikely she'd be seeing him again. He'd retreat back into his corner of the world, and she'd retreat into hers.

'Yes. Sorry, Glen, I seem to have driven one of our new volunteers away.'

Glen puffed out a breath. 'Forget about that. I'm just sorry to hear that it didn't work out for you. He seemed like a really nice guy.'

'He is. I'm just not a very nice girl.'

'Hey. None of that…' Glen frowned at her.

'I'll accept that it's a no fault on either side situation.'

'Okay. No fault on either side.' That at least allowed for some hope, even if it seemed unfair that two people who weren't at fault could manufacture such pain together.

'Bakewell tart? I saved you some.' Glen reached into the desk drawer and brought out a plastic box. 'Nothing better than Bakewell tart to mend a broken heart.'

That might be true in most circumstances. Sadly, Robbie felt it was going to take a little more than that to get over losing Joel.

'Thanks. My favourite. Can I save it for later?' She put the box next to her coffee cup. 'Shouldn't you be getting home soon? It's nearly eleven o'clock.'

Glen leaned back in his chair. 'Nah. Think I'll hang around a bit longer. Just in case you decide to tell me what the guy did to you to make you so miserable.'

Robbie shook her head. 'You may as well go. Joel didn't do anything, it was me. And I don't feel up to the details tonight. We'll do that another time.'

Glen shrugged, grabbing the phone when it rang, in a signal that he was staying anyway. Robbie took a sip of her coffee.

It really wasn't Joel's fault, however much

Glen wanted to jump to the conclusion that it must be. Joel might have disagreed with her and been appalled by the secrets she'd asked him to keep, but he'd never said that he didn't love her. He'd just said that he couldn't be with her.

Maybe that was the answer she'd been searching for. Joel had given her the self-confidence to step away from things that had hurt her, things she'd already held onto for too long. To be what she already knew herself to be. He'd never asked her to change because she didn't need to. She just needed to believe in him a little more.

The phone rang again, and Robbie reached for it.

'Hello, Nightshifters. How can we help?'

Joel had spent a lot of hours staring at the wall this weekend. Wishing that the world would just stop, because he didn't have any further use for it.

But it kept turning. Glen had been understanding when he'd called him and said he couldn't make it in this weekend and probably not any other weekend either. But he had to pitch up and do his shift in A & E because there would always be a queue of people who needed him there.

He'd wondered whether he'd see Robbie, even hoping that he might. He'd thought about how she might smile at him and how he'd have to smile back, because he'd never been able to ignore Robbie's smile. And then he'd thought about how he was hard-wired in a way that made it impossible to accept what she was asking of him. However much he understood, and however much he loved her.

But Robbie wasn't anywhere to be seen when he turned up to work on Monday evening. He'd done his best to make his enquiries as to her whereabouts sound casual, and heard that she'd been cleared to see patients now, and so was working back in the paediatric A & E unit.

It was all for the best. He went to see his supervisor and put in a request to work days for a while, which was readily accepted because he'd already worked more nights than were required of him. And then he gritted his teeth and got on with it.

The first weekend without her had been the worst—until the second came around. He had to find something to fill the void that she'd left, but that was difficult when everything he did reminded him of her.

He wept furious tears. And then, hidden deep inside, Joel found grief. Grief for his mother, and guilt for everything he'd done to shield her from the truth. The deeper he delved into his own heart, the more he missed Robbie, because she'd been his guide. He missed everything about her, the way she made him feel and the way he knew he made her feel. Her courage, her determination and the way she made him laugh. Her cooking...he even missed Robbie's cooking.

And then, on the third weekend, Robbie had led him to the place he should have gone to a long time ago. It was almost a year since Joel had seen his aunt Carrie and much longer than that since they'd really talked. When he'd called and asked if he might visit, she'd told him that he was welcome any time.

His uncle would be out with his sailing club on Saturday morning, and Aunt Carrie would be home on her own. She welcomed him with a hug, so like the ones his mother used to give.

He shouldn't think like that. Carrie wasn't a replacement for his mother, and she couldn't step in and forgive Joel in her stead. He was here for his aunt's sake, in the hopes that he could repair his relationship with her.

'Well.' Carrie settled down on the sofa opposite him. 'It's a treat to see my favourite nephew. What have I done to deserve a visit?'

He'd been away too long. Avoiding all of his

family so that he didn't have to confront the issues that hurt so much.

'I'm sorry. I should come more often.'

'You don't owe me anything, Joel. You come and go as you please.'

'I *wanted* to come more often, then, because I miss you.'

'That's nice to hear.' Carrie beamed at him. 'Your mother would have loved to see the way you've turned out. She was very proud that you were at medical school. She used to talk about it all the time.'

Familiar pain almost took his breath away. 'I didn't visit Mum as often as I should have, either.'

'Nonsense, Joel. You were studying and making a life for yourself. That's exactly what Theresa wanted for you.'

This was the opportunity he'd told himself he would take. 'I was wondering… Would you mind if we talked a bit about Mum?'

'No, of course not. You have something particular in mind?' Carrie leaned back in her seat, with the same expression she'd had on her face when he'd challenged her to board games when he was little. *Bring it on, kiddo.*

The secret hovered on the tip of his tongue. Instinctively Joel swallowed it back down, and it felt as if it were choking him.

But Carrie seemed to have none of his reservations. 'I don't suppose you've seen your father, have you? The last time I bumped into him, which was admittedly some time ago, he said you hadn't been in touch since Theresa died.'

'No. I haven't.'

'I'd be interested to know why that is, Joel. Your father said he had no clue, but I could tell that he knew a lot more than he was saying. He never was quite as clever as he thought.'

Carrie had asked, and he'd answer honestly; he owed her that much. 'A lot of reasons. One of them was that I didn't think he treated Mum very well.'

The silence in the room bore down on him like an oppressive mist. He and Carrie both opened their mouths to speak at the same time, and Joel smilingly indicated that she should go first.

'I think it's about time that we levelled with each other, don't you?'

He wanted to. Joel knew that he had to take the first step.

'Sometimes it's less hurtful to let the past stay where it is.' He should prepare Carrie for what was coming. Let her just nod her head in agreement, and drop the subject if she wanted to.

'I don't think so, Joel.' Carrie's mouth was quivering with emotion now. 'In my experience, pretending that things never happened doesn't make them go away.'

Carrie was right, and she'd issued him with an ultimatum. Whatever the consequences, whether or not his aunt could accept what he'd done, Joel had to tell the truth.

'I found out that my father was having an affair, when I was seven. He swore me to secrecy, saying it was for Mum's sake because the family would break up if I said anything...' He felt himself flinch as Carrie's hand flew to her mouth. 'Carrie, I'm so sorry.'

'Oh, my goodness. You *knew*?'

'Did you?'

'Yes, your mother told me. You know she had a habit of thinking the best of everyone, especially your father, but she wasn't stupid. She used to come round and drink tea and tell me that she loved your father and that it would all blow over. No one would know that anything was ever the matter...'

Suddenly everything was coming into sharp focus. Joel was finally beginning to see it all through an adult's eyes, and not a child's.

'I'm pretty sure that Andrew didn't know—he was only two years old. I did, though. My father used to take me out in the afternoon and leave me in the park to play on my own for hours. When he got back, he'd tell me that I had to tell Mum that we'd been together the whole time.' Joel shrugged. 'I never told her. I felt very guilty about that.'

A tear dribbled down Carrie's cheek. 'That never should have been allowed to happen. *I* should never have allowed it to happen.'

Joel shrugged numbly. What had all of his guilt and soul-searching been for? 'There was no way you could have known. No way that Mum could have known.'

'Theresa was my sister, and you know how much I loved her. How much I still do love her… But I should have realised that a lot of what she said was just wishful thinking. You never should have had to bear that burden.'

Joel got to his feet, moving over to the sofa to sit next to Carrie. When he put his arm around her shaking shoulders, trying to comfort her, she clung to him, crying. 'I'm so sorry, Joel.'

He knew now exactly what to say. Robbie had shown him the way and given him the strength to take that path.

'Carrie, listen. This was never my fault and it was never yours. We got caught up in something that wasn't of our making. It's not too late for either of us to make our peace with that.'

They talked for a long time. He stayed for dinner and when he left Carrie hugged him and demanded that they make a date for dinner at his house. His uncle's parting words to him convinced him that he'd done the right thing.

'Thank you for coming, Joel. Carrie's been needing to talk about this, for a long time.'

Robbie was nervous. Actually, nervous didn't cover it.

Glen helped her write the press release, striking out all of the parts he said were too apologetic, and replacing them with a succinct history of how Nightshifters had been founded. Robbie added short profiles of Glen and the members of the board, and details of the expansion plans.

'There. That'll do. When we actually get around to releasing it, we'll add a couple of case studies. But the Nightshifters don't need those, they just want to know what's happening.'

'And what I've done.' Robbie pulled an agonised face.

'What you've done is to build something we're all proud of, Rob, and it's about time you took some credit for it. Going public is the best way to expand, and we're ready to do that now. We're telling our own crew first, so they don't read it in the papers later on.'

Robbie wondered if the Nightshifters would see it the same way. But she emailed a copy of the press release to each of the volunteers along with an invitation to a meeting at the Tin Tabernacle.

By the evening of the meeting she was feeling sick with worry. Carla had said she'd be there, which meant that two people would be talking to her, at least. The Tin Tabernacle was filling up quickly, and Roy popped in to announce that he was back and feeling in the best of health, accepting a plate of sausage rolls from the food and drinks table to take back to the boats.

Then Glen roared for silence, and everyone sat down on the rows of chairs that had been put out.

'All right. I don't need to tell you what's going on, you've all had the information by email, and the plans for Oxford are over there on the wall. So I'll go straight to questions and comments.'

Glen sat down again. Robbie would have preferred that he'd talked a little longer, but he was right. Everyone had the information, and this meeting was about their thoughts and ideas. Saying anything more was just putting off the moment that Robbie was dreading.

Rosie stood up, brandishing her copy of the press release. 'I want to propose a motion.'

'Sure. Knock yourself out, Rosie.' Glen nodded.

This was it. Rosie had been a good friend over the years, and she didn't mince her words. Losing her now, losing any of the people here, would tear Robbie's heart out. But they deserved to know.

'If I'd been financing this place, I'd make sure everyone knew about it...' Heads nodded in agreement. 'But Robbie just went ahead and did it. I don't know about you, but I'm pretty fed up about that.'

Here it came. Rosie was clearly working up to a sting in the tail, which was exactly what Robbie deserved. She felt herself flush with misery.

'So I'm going to put things right. I'm proposing a vote of thanks to Robbie, for everything here that means so much to so many people. And for being a complete dunderhead, because she didn't sit back and reckon she'd done enough already, but pitched in and worked as hard as any of us.'

'Yep!' Glen's hand went up, but it wasn't the first. Hands were being raised thick and fast, and Robbie felt tears of relief spring to her eyes. Glen stood up and tried to count them, and then gave up.

'I think that's unanimous. Apart from Carla...' He shot his wife a querying look.

'Oh. Do I get a vote as well?'

A groan ran around the hall and Rosie spoke up again. 'Carla gets two votes. On account of the mince pies, last Christmas.'

Carla beamed at Rosie and held up two hands.

'Right, then. Consider yourself well and truly thanked, Robbie, and thank you to Rosie for proposing our first motion.' Glen turned to Robbie mouthing, *I told you so.* 'Now, let's settle down and have some questions about the expansion, shall we?'

There was a lively discussion about the new branch of Nightshifters, and quite a few good ideas. Glen was taking notes and fielding the questions, and Robbie sat still and silent. Carla slipped from her seat and came to sit next to her.

'You okay?'

'Yes. Thanks. I'm just a bit overwhelmed.'

Carla nodded. 'You deserve it. Does this make a difference to you?'

Robbie thought for a moment. She'd be going to Oxfordshire tomorrow for two weeks, and when she got back the press release would go out. Joel might still be too angry with her to take any heed of it, but even if she never saw him again, she'd know that his love and hers hadn't been for nothing, because it had brought her to this point. She'd done it for him, and for herself and for the Nightshifters. And if she did see Joel again, she could at least look him in the eye, and tell him that she'd done her best to be worthy of his love.

'Yes. It makes all the difference in the world.'

Change was hard. It had its good times, being able to phone Carrie and talk when he wanted to, and hearing that she'd been in touch with his brother, Andrew, and that he'd asked after Joel. It would take time, and maybe Andrew would never know about what he'd been too young to understand, but Joel was beginning to see a possibility of change.

And it had its bad times. Waking up in the night and reaching for Robbie was the worst of them, because the cruel disappointment when he remembered that she wasn't there was like losing her all over again.

Joel didn't dare try to see her, but he was hungry for news of Robbie. And the gossip he overheard from the hospital grapevine was always happy to oblige.

'I heard that Nightshifters are expanding their operation and setting up another office in Oxford.'

'I heard that too. Good thing, I'd say. And David Hampton-Hall is involved with the project. I didn't know he was Robbie's father, did you...?'

'I don't think anyone knew. You've got to respect her for keeping quiet about it and not trying to trade on her family name. By the way, did you know that Josie's gone over to Paeds for three weeks?'

'No. I knew she wanted to make the move.'

'It's just temporary, she's filling in while Robbie's on leave. But at least Josie will be getting some experience there, and it'll stand her in good stead if she applies for a transfer...'

Robbie was moving on. No...she was moving out, coming out of hiding and spreading her wings. And if he'd needed any reason to remind himself that he still loved her, it was the warmth that he felt at that thought. Almost in a daze, he went to his supervisor and asked if he might have a week's leave, to deal with an urgent personal matter. And when his request was granted, he knew what he had to do.

He drove home and fell into bed, bone weary from so many sleepless nights. He slept for fourteen hours, then woke with the kind of resolve that he hadn't felt in a while.

He needed coffee, lots of it. Plenty of carbs, some stretching exercises, and a map of Oxfordshire. Then, ninety-two phone calls later, he hit gold.

'Good afternoon, The Cloisters Hotel.'

'Hi. Olivia Hampton-Hall, please.'

A pause. Joel lay on the sofa, staring at the ceiling and replaying the inevitable answer in his head. Always starting with *I'm sorry*...

'May I take a message, sir?'

Joel sat up suddenly, scattering crumbs and knocking his cup over. Robbie was capable of disappearing from his life, but she just didn't have it in her DNA to stay completely out of reach, in case someone from Nightshifters needed her. He'd reckoned that she would probably be out all day working, and that she would have instructed the hotel's reception to take messages.

'No, I'll catch her later. Thank you.'

He grabbed the map. He'd painstakingly worked his way out from the centre of Oxford, calling every hotel he could find. The Cloisters Hotel, was a little over eight miles from his starting point, and now he knew where Robbie was. Tracing his finger across the map, from London to Oxford, made the distance between them seem inconsequential. Tomorrow he'd be facing a much more difficult journey.

CHAPTER THIRTEEN

JOEL WAS UP early and on the road before nine o'clock. He got stuck in traffic in West London, and then the day became bright and clear, with an open road in front of him. The Cloisters Hotel was just outside Oxford, and it lived up to its name.

The main reception area was modern and sleek, complementing the old stone arches that he could see at the far end, which revealed a carefully kept courtyard garden beyond. It was quiet, the kind of place you'd go if you were searching for respite. Joel had the uncomfortable feeling that respite was exactly what Robbie had been searching for, and that it was from him.

'Olivia Hampton-Hall, please.'

The receptionist's lips moved automatically into a professional smile. 'May I take a message, sir?'

'No, that's okay, I really need to see her. Do you know when she'll be back?'

'I can pass on a message...' That was clearly all the receptionist was authorised to do.

'I'll call her. Thanks.' Joel wondered whether sitting in Reception and waiting for her was the thing to do, and decided that he might be there all day. Not that he'd mind, but it might elicit a few questions.

He went back out to his car, and got in. It made sense to just wait until Robbie returned to the hotel. It actually made sense to wait until she returned to London, but he had no idea when that would be or even if she was going to be back. She didn't have to consider the practicalities of a place to live and a job—her trust fund meant that she could just leave everything behind and disappear if she wanted to, and Joel feared that this was exactly what she was doing.

But Robbie was practical. The hotel was nice—gorgeous actually—but she was perfectly capable of staying anywhere as long as it was close to where she needed to be. He had to just trust in what he knew and think. If Robbie was setting up a new regional office for Nightshifters it would be somewhere near one of the major routes into the surrounding towns. Probably somewhere that satisfied her fascination with the unusual and her commitment to communities...

Fifteen minutes later, he threw his phone back down onto the passenger seat and started the engine. It was only a ten-minute drive, and as soon as he turned off the main road and onto the newly tarmacked lane he knew he was in the right place.

Tin Chapel Field was right ahead of him. And although there was no Tin Tabernacle there, there was a new structure that resembled one, with the same arched wooden doors and wooden-framed windows. The walls and roof looked as if the original corrugated iron had been replaced with a modern high-performance material that wasn't quite so susceptible to rust as the Tin Tabernacle in London. But at a distance the two looked much the same, apart from the fact that this one was sky blue. Joel stopped the car on the paved parking area, next to three others.

He walked over to a man who was perched on a ladder, painting the wooden eaves. 'Hi. Is Robbie around?'

'You've just missed her.' The man put one last finishing touch to the bright, white gloss and climbed down the ladder. 'She won't be long. She's gone to fetch lunch.'

That was just like Robbie. She didn't care

about being the boss, she just did whatever was useful. The thought prompted a wave of intense yearning, coupled with terror at this uncertain enterprise, and Joel choked both back.

'Nice place…' He nodded towards the building and the man beamed.

'Yeah, it's come out all right. Took us three days to put it up. It came in a flat pack from the manufacturers.'

'There used to be one like it here?'

The man laughed. 'The Tin Chapel rusted away years ago, terrible old thing it was. The name survived, though. It's nice that there's going to be something like it here again.'

And this place was an ideal location, both beautiful and practical. There was easy access to a main road, but it was surrounded by open fields.

'Plenty of space.' Joel was trying not to think about beautiful and practical, because those were words he connected with Robbie, and his heart might tear into little pieces, right here and now.

'Yeah, the land goes right down to that boundary there.' The man pointed towards a fence that circled a wide area of grass, along with copses of trees and what looked like a small stream.

The sound of a car approaching made them

both turn. Robbie looked as if she might be about to ram his car with hers, but at the last moment she reversed, parking on the other side of the paving. No doubt she'd seen sense and decided that when she told him to go, he was going to need some form of transport.

Joel swallowed hard, trying not to think about it. In his determination to find her, he'd been able to put aside thoughts about what was going to happen when he actually did find her, but now he was facing the biggest challenge of his life.

She got out of the car, reaching in to collect a cardboard tray of drinks and a large carrier bag. The sunshine reflected in her hair as she walked towards him and surprisingly she didn't have a scowl on her face. But it was possible that was just for the benefit of the man standing beside him. Another couple of men had appeared at the door of the building and Robbie handed over the lunches and watched them walk away towards an old picnic table that had been set up on the grass. When she turned, her face was grave.

'How did you know I was here?'

That hurt, because it meant that Robbie must have deliberately covered her tracks, so that he couldn't find her. He gestured towards the grass on the other side of the building, out of sight of the workmen. If she was going to punch him, then he really didn't need anyone to rush over and save him, because it was what he deserved. And if he was going to get down on his knees and beg, he'd rather do it without the distraction of an audience.

She walked to the spot he'd indicated and then turned to face him.

'What is it, Joel?'

Not being able to believe that this was really Joel, when she'd first caught sight of him, was less to do with the realities of the situation, and more to do with what had been going on in Robbie's head. She'd thought about him. Dreamed about him. Once, the hairs on the back of her neck had prickled, when she'd thought she'd caught his scent, but when she'd looked round he wasn't there. Hallucinations weren't such a big step away from that, even if they were a concern.

But you couldn't hallucinate this. The way he stood, the fine balance of his body and the way he smiled as he chatted to Dave. It had been something akin to the shock she'd felt when she'd been catapulted off her bike and hit the ground, and in her consternation she'd almost rammed her car into his. Robbie had wiped the tears from her eyes, picked up the lunches and faced him, but she was trembling all over.

She wrapped her jacket around her, folding her arms across her stomach. Maybe that would keep her in one piece for a while.

'What is it, Joel?'

'I'm sorry. Truly sorry.'

He looked sorry. She was sorry too, but Robbie couldn't bring herself to believe that it would change anything. The press release hadn't even been sent yet, so there was no way that he could know what she'd done.

'Apology accepted.'

'What?' That was clearly the last thing he'd expected her to say. And the sudden flash of warmth in his eyes made her want to cry.

'I said things I regret too.' Maybe she should tell him that there were no more secrets any more. Or maybe she should wait, and let him say what he wanted to say first.

He nodded, looking down at the grass. 'You had every right to say what you said.'

This was harder than she'd thought it would be. How could he stand there, looking so beautiful, and not realise how agonising this was?

'Is that all you wanted to say, Joel?'

His jaw hardened. 'I wouldn't have come all this way if there was nothing more to say. If I felt the same as I did then...'

So what's changed? Robbie couldn't get the words out, she just stared at him dumbly. Something at the back of her mind was insisting furiously that if this was the last time she would see him, she wanted every second of it to keep, because however awful things were between them, it was better than being without him.

'I went to see Aunt Carrie… We talked for a long time.'

So he was finding some healing. That was good. She'd found some too, but maybe what she'd done wasn't going to be enough for him…

'I've realised something. Neither of us can change what happened in the past, but we can change how we choose to deal with it.'

'I…' Robbie hardly dared say anything. If this sounded too good to be true it probably was, but Joel was here, and that must mean something.

'I'm sorry too. You were right, I shouldn't have asked you to keep my secrets. I'm doing my best to leave them behind.'

He smiled suddenly. 'I heard. Hospital gossip's got a lot to say about Nightshifters and how you turned out to be David Hampton-Hall's daughter. Robbie, I'm not asking you to come back to me…'

There it was. It *was* too good to be true after all. Disappointment tore at her savagely, and then suddenly Joel fell to his knees. Robbie jumped back, yelping in surprise.

'I love you, and I'm asking you to talk to me. Just to find out whether we can work through this, because I really believe that we can leave the past behind and find a future.'

'Joel. Get up.' She could feel tears on her cheeks.

'So I can walk away from you?' He shook his head. 'Sorry, Robbie, not a chance. Not this time. If there's any walking to be done, then you'll have to do it.'

That was just fine, because Joel was the best thing that had ever happened to her, and she'd never leave him. She flung herself at him, hugging him awkwardly.

He was trembling too. Holding onto her as if she was the one and only thing he'd ever wanted. Robbie wasn't sure how long her legs were going to hold her, and she pulled away from him, dropping to her knees.

Better. He could hold her and kiss her now, the way she wanted him to, and he did just that.

'Please, Joel. Tell me you mean this…'

He dropped back onto his heels, holding her hands between his.

'I love you, Robbie. I'll do everything to prove that to you—'

'Just tell me. Then I'll know I can believe it.'

'I mean it.'

'I love you too, Joel. I mean it.' This felt like a lasting promise, one that opened up a future for them both.

He grinned. 'Will you come on a date with me, then?'

That would be perfect. She wanted to share everything with Joel and the one thing they hadn't had time for was a romantic first date.

'Yes.'

'Now?'

Now was going to be a problem…

'I really want to. But Dad's been helping out with some of the fundraising and publicity and he and Mum are driving down to see how the Tin Tabernacle's going, and take some photographs. They'll be here in a couple of hours…' She reached forward, trying to smooth the look of sudden panic on Joel's face.

'They'll love you. Not as much as I do, but…'

He grinned. 'I can face the terrors of being introduced to your parents. As long as you love me.'

'I do. But if I'm going to introduce you to them, we'll have to be going steady. At least.'

That wicked look that she loved so much

crept into his smile. 'You're right. Going steady it is, then. Officially.'

Robbie had wondered aloud whether going back to the hotel, for an hour alone before her parents arrived, would be possible and Joel had vetoed the idea. Clearly he felt that frustrated yearning was a better look than smug satisfaction when greeting her parents, and perhaps he was right. Although, that hadn't stopped him from accompanying her on a tour around the land attached to the new Tin Tabernacle, when he knew full well that as soon as they were out of sight of the workmen and among the trees they'd be kissing and making all of the promises that Robbie so wanted to hear.

Her dad liked him. What wasn't to like? Joel was affable and smiling and knew a lot about some of the medical issues that her dad's charities were involved with. Before long the two men were taking a stroll around the boundaries of the property, talking animatedly together. Her mother joined her at the window of the Tin Tabernacle as she stared out at them.

'Don't look so worried, Robbie. They'll manage if you take your eye off them for one minute.'

They probably would, but then that would

be one minute that Robbie missed out on. 'You think Dad likes him?'

'That would make any difference?'

'Yes, because I want them to like each other. No, because *I* like him.'

Her mother laughed. 'Yes. I can see that. Of course your father likes him. Joel's clearly devoted to you, and that's a very good start. His being a doctor gives them something to talk about, and… Ah, yes. See, they're pacing out the area for the new community centre…'

Dad was gesturing to show the scale of the proposed building, and Joel was nodding, obviously asking a few questions. Robbie had been otherwise occupied when they'd reached the trees that would surround the community centre, and had forgotten to mention it to Joel.

'Is there a nice pub near here?' her mother asked.

'Yes, there are loads of them.'

'Good. I could do with a G & T and a sandwich before we go.'

Robbie hid the smile that sprang to her lips behind her hand, not wishing to give the impression that she didn't want to see her parents. 'I thought you were staying for dinner at the hotel.'

Her mother frowned. 'For goodness' sakes, Robbie. I'll be happy with a thank you, for taking your father off back to London while you do whatever it is you're impatient to do with that young man of yours. I don't blame you, he's rather gorgeous.'

Mum had never talked like that about any of her boyfriends. But then none of her boyfriends had been Joel.

'Thanks, Mum. We'll do dinner another time. Very soon.'

Joel wasn't due to go back to work for another week, and their time together here had been idyllic. Working hard during the day, at the new Tin Tabernacle, and playing hard and sweet at night. Robbie was happy and that was really all that Joel cared about, because she never failed to make him happy.

He'd promised to take her on the belated 'first date' on the Saturday evening before he left and the hotel's conservatory-style restaurant was the perfect place. Robbie was in the bathroom, getting ready, and Joel was pacing their hotel room.

'What are you doing?' She appeared in the doorway, in a sleeveless blue and white dress that fell softly around her legs. Her hair was pinned up in an artfully messy arrangement at the back of her head, and her smile was the most beautiful thing he'd ever seen.

'Pacing. Isn't that what you're supposed to do on a first date?' He came to a halt. 'You look gorgeous. It's a nice dress, as well.'

She laughed, pleased with the compliment. Robbie didn't much care about things but she cared about people. And she knew that this particular person belonged to her, and always would.

'You look particularly delicious, too. Very undressable.' She looked around the room. 'Have you seen my shoes? The blue suede ones.'

'Under the bed. Let me get them for you.'

'My Prince Charming. How many phone calls was it to find me again?' Robbie plumped herself down onto the bed.

'More than two.' Joel reached under the bed, grabbing her shoes.

'I heard you scoured the kingdom for me. Followed the clues to the Tin Tabernacle.' She grinned, holding her foot out.

'Not really. I had the advantage of an online map.' He dropped her suede court shoe over her toes. 'Too bad. It doesn't fit.'

Robbie pulled a face of mock horror, reaching for her foot and pulling the shoe on.

'Yes, it does.'

'Well, that's a relief. May I kiss you now, princess?'

Now. He'd been planning to do this later, but he was already on his knees in front of her and he just couldn't wait any longer. Earlier in the week, Joel had driven back to London to fetch some clothes and drop some papers that Robbie had signed in to the charity's solicitor. He had used the opportunity for a more important errand. He'd gone from shop to shop, knowing that he couldn't afford the kind of ring that Robbie really deserved, and then he'd come to his senses. She didn't want the sizeable rocks that he'd been wishing he could buy her; Robbie would find such a thing bulky and impractical.

She'd told him that she wanted his love, and he'd promised she'd always have it. And when he'd found a jeweller who would put the stones of his choice into an eternity ring and then courier it down to the hotel, he'd thought carefully about what he wanted to say to her.

He kissed her, a little nervous now. But love could do anything it wanted, it had brought them back together, and sealed their whispered promises. It could do this, too.

'Olivia Roberta Hampton-Hall…'

She smiled at him. '*All* my names. I'm listening carefully.'

'Good start. I never had a choice about falling in love with you, but it *is* my choice to love you a little more each day. Will you marry me?'

'Joel. Yes!' Robbie squealed with delight, throwing her arms around his shoulders. Joel resisted the impulse to stay like this, just kissing her, and felt in his pocket for the ring.

'I have this…'

She looked down at the ring, resting in the palm of his hand. 'Oh! Joel, it's beautiful. Aquamarine…'

'For the colour of your eyes in the sunlight.'

'And sapphires…'

Joel smiled. 'The colour of your eyes after dark. Diamonds for the promises we make, and platinum for the strength to keep them.'

'And in an unbroken circle for eternity. Joel, this is so perfect.'

She laid her hand in his and he put the ring onto her finger. Different shades of blue, blending together as she turned her hand in the light. Robbie took a moment to look at it, and then cupped her fingers over her ear.

'I can hear it, Joel. Everything it's saying to me.'

He couldn't stop smiling. Joel held her tight, feeling her heart beating against his.

'Are you ready for our first date?'

When Robbie turned her gaze up towards his, her eyes were as blue as the sapphires on her finger, promising him everything for the night ahead. Everything for the rest of their lives.

'Yes. I do believe I am.'

EPILOGUE

ONE YEAR. ONE WEDDING. One baby. One true love who would never let her down.

Robbie sat in the garden of their new house in Oxfordshire, watching Joel with their eight-week-old son. Daniel seemed to be growing by the day, and she'd never seen Joel so happy.

'They'll be here soon. Why don't you give Daniel to me?'

'In a minute…'

'Now, Joel. Stop monopolising him. I'm sure I haven't had my share of cuddles this morning.'

Joel came to sit next to her on the bench, curling his arm around her and holding Daniel between them. 'Will that do? I can't let go of him just yet. You get all day to hold him when I'm at work.'

'This is good. Two for the price of one.' Robbie kissed him. 'And don't tell me that you don't love your new job.'

Joel chuckled. 'I love my new job. Not as much as you and Daniel, and it's less of a challenge, but I do love it?'

'*Less* of a challenge? Making your mark as head of A & E in a brand-new hospital? Moving down here three weeks before Daniel was born? I'm pleased and proud to be more of a challenge than that,' Robbie teased him.

'Always. You'll always be my first and best challenge.'

A car drew up on the hard standing beside the house. 'He's here, Joel. Your next challenge.'

Joel nodded. 'I'm still not sure what I'm going to say to him.'

'*Hello* will do for starters. Then you introduce him and his wife to your wife and son, and then you show them around the garden, while I cook lunch.'

'I was thinking about doing the cooking myself.' Joel leaned over and kissed her. 'I can do something quick and easy for today, and tomorrow, when we have the place to ourselves, we can let rip and you can devastate our new kitchen.'

Robbie chuckled. 'I'm looking forward to it already. In that case, you men can share culinary tips, and Daniel and I will be on garden duty.'

'And then?' Joel's brow creased.

'And then you take everything as it comes. You don't have to even think about the past, because we have a future to concentrate on.'

'Yeah. Thanks. I needed to hear that one more time.'

Robbie watched as Joel got to his feet, walking across the grass to the car. A man and a woman were getting out, and the woman hung back while the man strode forward to meet Joel. There was one moment of hesitation and then the rather formal handshake turned into a bear hug. Robbie let out a sigh of relief.

'There, Daniel, see that?' Daniel seemed half asleep now, and he hadn't seen anything.

But Robbie had seen it. Aunt Carrie's diplomacy and Joel's careful determination had borne fruit and Joel had finally got to hug his brother again.

* * * * *

If you enjoyed this story, check out these other great reads from Annie Claydon

Risking It All for a Second Chance
The Doctor's Reunion to Remember
Falling for the Brooding Doc
Greek Island Fling to Forever

All available now!